BLAZING SIX-GUNS

A band of horsemen burst over the small ridge and swept down on the ranch house, bellowing like savages and firing rifles. Morgan caught up his Spencer repeating rifle and bellied down behind some light brush as he levered a round into the chamber.

Then Buckskin saw two men stop their mounts and light torches. He got off his first shot too fast. It drilled through the neck of one man's horse, sending the animal off in a wild, bucking spate that unseated the cowboy and pitched him to the ground. Morgan took better aim on the second man and thundered his round into the man's upper chest, pivoting him off the mount.

Morgan grinned and waited....

Also in the *Buckskin* Series:

BUCKSKIN #39

BLAZING SIX-GUNS

KIT DALTON

LEISURE BOOKS NEW YORK CITY

A LEISURE BOOK®

June 2006

Published by

Dorchester Publishing Co., Inc.
200 Madison Avenue
New York, NY 10016

ISBN 0-8439-3611-8

The name "Leisure Books" and the stylized "L" with design are trademarks of Dorchester Publishing Co., Inc.

Printed in the United States of America.

Chapter One

Buckskin Lee Morgan sat on his bay mare in the fringes of a softly chattering creek that cut across the spring-green landscape less than two-hundred yards from the ranch house, barns and small buildings of a modest sized cattle spread. He hadn't wanted to get any closer.

Spade Bit Ranch.

The name haunted him now as it had for the past ten years. This once had been where he grew up, the Spade Bit Ranch. The old ranch house was gone, burned down, he remembered, from some distant past message. This was where he had been born and lived with his father so many years ago. Good times and bad. He couldn't remember his mother or when she left.

He stared at the place again. No sense going up to the house. He wouldn't know the people there. He'd sold the place a dozen years ago when

5

the sheriff had trumped up some charges against him and had the nerve to put out a wanted poster. He'd heard the old homestead had gone through different hands since. A horse ranch wasn't an easy way to make a living.

Buckskin took one last long look at the place, the rise of ground behind the barn, the well house, the corrals. Most of them were intact. He saw a cowhand bring a pair of horses out of the corral and head toward the house.

A rifle shot boomed into the silence. One of the horses the hand led went down with a scream of lethal volume. The hand dropped the reins and sprinted for the barn twenty yards away. Dust kicked up around his feet twice; then he was in the safety of the building.

Buckskin had automatically drawn his Colt from right thigh leather and looked to see from where the shot had come. At the same time, a band of horsemen burst over the small ridge a quarter of a mile to the north and swept down on the ranch house bellowing like savages and firing rifles at the buildings.

Buckskin dropped off his bay, caught his Spencer repeating rifle on his way and bellied down behind some light brush as he levered a round into the chamber. He picked the lead rider who had his long gun blazing, led him a little and fired. The .52-caliber Spencer round jolted into the rider's side, heart high, and he folded up like a rag puppy, slammed off the far side of his horse and fell to the ground, dead in an instant.

The other riders kept going, swept around the ranch house and broke every window in the place with six-gun rounds. Buckskin saw two men stop their mounts and light torches. The ranch house's roof would be dry this time of year and burn like pine tar.

Buckskin got off his first shot too fast. It drilled through the neck of the torch man's horse, sending it off in a wild bucking spate that unseated the cowboy and pitched him to the ground. He dropped his torch and ran after his horse.

The second fire man got his torch burning furiously. Coal oil-soaked rags, Buckskin figured. The long, lean rifleman on the ground under the brush took better aim this time and thundered his next round into the torch man's upper chest, pivoting him off his mount and grounding the torch.

The eight other riders had circled the house, and now headed for the barn, but when they saw two of their men on the ground they looked around for the shooter. Buckskin grinned. The slight breeze blew in his face and it had drifted the white smoke from his rounds backwards into the brush along the creek. The riders below couldn't see it when it came out the top of the greenery broken up into a million small puffs of slightly colored smoke.

Buckskin waited.

The eight men below rode behind the barn and evidently had a gab session. Gunfire came from one of the broken windows in the house but the last man scurried farther behind the barn and out of the field of fire.

After a minute, the eight riders rode straight away from the barn, keeping it between them and the house. Soon they were in Buckskin's view so he pumped four more shots at them, emptying the tube of rounds in the Spencer. He had two more loaded tubes in the boot, but figured he wouldn't need them. A few minutes later the last of the raiders topped the rise a quarter of a mile beyond the barns and was gone.

Buckskin heard someone shouting and saw the last man he shot lift one hand. Someone looked out the back screen door. The face vanished. A moment later a woman came out the door holding a shotgun and advanced on the downed barn burner. She walked up to the man warily, kicked away what must have been his six-gun, then lay down the shotgun and knelt in the dust of the yard beside the wounded man.

The screen door slammed and a man walked out holding revolvers in both hands. He evidently said something to the woman, who replied and looked over her shoulder, then went back to ministering to the wounded man.

Buckskin couldn't figure it. He reloaded the Spencer with a fresh tube of seven shots, chambered a round and caught his horse's reins. He walked out of the brush holding the Spencer over his head in a sign of friendship.

He was 50 yards away before they saw him. He called out.

"Hello, the ranch. I'm on your side. Don't shoot."

The girl stood quickly, brought the shotgun around to cover him as he advanced. He ignored the threat, lowered the rifle and put it in the leather boot attached to his saddle, then continued to walk forward.

As he came closer he saw the man step behind the woman. He had put one six-gun in his belt, but still held the other in his left hand with the muzzle pointed at his boots.

The girl gradually lowered the shotgun. She was young, maybe nineteen, he figured. Her cheap gingham dress was soiled from the yard dirt. It pinched in at her waist, flared dramatically over her breasts, and extended to her throat. The sleeves went down to her wrists. Her hair was dark and unfashionably short. As he came closer he could see her dark eyes in a solemn face.

"You the shooter in the brush who helped us?" the girl asked. He was surprised at her breathy not-quite-finished voice.

"Yes, Miss. Figured you could use some help."

"Thanks, we're not much of a hand with guns. Pa said we didn't need to be."

"Your pa here?"

She looked up and tears spilled from her eyes. She wiped at them shaking her head at the same time. "Oh, no. He died near six months ago. Don't seem real yet."

"I'm sorry."

He hesitated. He hadn't looked at the man. Now he did and saw a boy no more than twenty. Not a man in anything but size. He was five-ten, medium build but his mannerisms and his expression were of someone much younger.

The girl brushed off her skirt. She pointed at the man on the ground. "He's hurt bad. We should get him into the house."

"He just tried to burn you out," Buckskin said. "Now you're going to nurse him?"

"Of course. It's what any normal person would

do. Will you help us get him onto the front porch?"

Buckskin nodded. He knelt beside the wounded man. The round had made a nasty entry wound that bled over half his shirt. It must have gone on through and out his back.

"Can you hear me?" he asked the man on the ground.

"Yes."

"Why did you attack the ranch?"

"Orders. Boss said burn you to the ground."

"Who is the boss?"

"They're from the Black Kettle Ranch just south of us," the girl said. "They want our water rights."

Buckskin motioned for the man behind the girl to catch the man's legs. Buckskin picked up the raider and he bellowed in pain, then passed out. The two carried the unconscious man to the shaded and screened front porch where the girl had a cot ready for him.

She brought a pan of cold water and a cloth and bathed his face until he regained consciousness. Buckskin took one of the dry cloths she had brought and made a compress of it which he pressed against the bullet's ugly exit wound to stop some of the bleeding.

"What's your name?" the girl asked the wounded man.

"Don't matter. Know I'm dying. Damned shame dying for a bastard like Lombard." He gasped and blood showed at his lips. He wheezed, closed his eyes a moment, then opened them and looked at the girl.

"Mitzi, never had nothing against you. Just

10

doing what the boss told me to. Damn, that hurts!" His eyes went wide, he lifted one hand and then a long scream came from his throat. When it ended his head rolled to one side.

"He's dead," Buckskin said.

The girl blinked back tears as she rose from where she had knelt by the cot. "The early death of any human being is a tragedy," she said. She went to sit on the steps.

Buckskin stood in front of her. "My name is Buckskin Lee Morgan. I was passing by, figured I'd take a look at the old home place. I used to own this spread. We called it the Spade Bit Ranch back then."

She brushed back tears and stood. "Yes, I remember the Spade Bit Ranch name. I grew up in town. My father bought this place five years ago. Turned it into a cattle spread. Oh, pardon me."

Her hands went to her face for a moment, then she held out one hand. "I'm Mitzi Roland, and that's my brother Claude on the porch. We're trying best we can to run this ranch. I'm afraid we're not doing a good job of it. I don't know much about ranching. Pa was doing fine here, but then he took a fever and a day later he died. We're kind of struggling."

"The Black Kettle riders do this kind of raiding often?"

"Oh, no. This is the first time they've shot at the ranch house itself. A month ago, they burned down a small barn. Next day, Isaiah Lombard himself came rolling up in his fancy buggy and offered to buy our ranch. I ran him off with a

11

shotgun blast over his head. Pa did teach me how to shoot.

"Good thing, since Claude isn't good with guns." She grimaced. "Fact is, Claude isn't much good at anything. We had a great foreman, knew cattle, new this land. Then Lombard bought him away from us for seventy-five dollars a month and found."

Mitzi looked up at him, then down at the .45 tied low on his leg. "I don't understand. You're a stranger to us. Why did you mix in?"

Buckskin sat down on the porch step and she sat down three feet from him.

"Kinda trying to figure that out myself. Old home place is partly it. Then I saw ten men with guns attack a ranch, it didn't seem right. I wasn't sure anyone else was here. They did try to gun down your hand from ambush. I guess that was it. I hate bushwhackers."

"Makes sense." She stared at him.

He watched her eyes that he could now tell were brown. They evaluated him. She had a round, happy face, with a dimple that poked in on her left cheek now and then when she smiled. Her nose was short but tipped up and interesting. Mitzi's mouth was full with slightly pouting lips over a firm chin and a tight, trim neck vanishing into her blouse. He wouldn't let himself stare at her breasts.

"Mr. Morgan, you any good with cattle?"

"Earned my keep that way more than once."

"Want a job ramroding my huge crew of four hands? This is the Box R Ranch and last count we had two-hundred brood cows, one-hundred head of steer ready to market, another three-hundred steers growing up, and enough range bulls to do the job. The pay is—" She stopped. "Pay is forty dollars a month and found. Most I can afford. If you don't want the job, I understand."

"Depends on a few things. Is Brittenhauser still the sheriff here?"

"Don't recall the name. Lombard is the sheriff now, same coyote who owns the Black Kettle below us. Isaiah Lombard, elected by the people and Lombard's crooked ballot counters two years ago."

Buckskin grinned. The girl had more spunk and fire than he had figured. "I'd guess you don't like Sheriff Lombard."

"I don't like him or his son."

"Another problem. Twelve years ago there was a spurious wanted poster out on me from the former sheriff. Have you ever seen one and do you know if it still exists?"

She shook her head. "Not that I know of, but I don't look over wanted posters often."

"You say that the Black Kettle riders have been harassing you lately. Is it a concentrated try to drive you off the land?"

"Yes. Ever since Lombard tried to buy me out at a far, far too low a price. But who can I go to? Lombard is the sheriff."

"You need to go to the Territorial Attorney General. He should be here in Boise."

"Oh, yes. I hadn't thought about that." She turned to him and smiled. "Mr. Morgan, I truly hope that you can help us out here by being our foreman. I need somebody who can stand up to Lombard and his bullies. Claude just isn't able to do it."

13

"How are your finances? Do you need to get those hundred head of steers to the market soon?"

"Overdue for market. I'm short on cash. I sold twenty head to a small packinghouse in Boise. Now I need to get those hundred head on the train. We have a spur line into Boise now. We tried to make a drive two weeks ago, but some mystery riders hit us and scattered the herd. They were from the Black Kettle I'm sure, but I can't prove it."

He nodded. "Miss Roland, I'll take the job, at least until we get things straightened out for you. Two conditions. First, you call me Buckskin. Second, I have to spend a day in Boise first to find out what my status is here now. I'd hate to go to work for you just to get arrested and hung."

Her eyes went wide and her hand came to her mouth. "Oh, dear, no!" She frowned slightly and then nodded. "Yes, I can call you Buckskin, and you call me Mitzi. Of course you can go into town and check on matters."

"Who in Boise can I trust? Who is a good friend of yours there?"

"The saddlemaker, Harry Blackhawk. I almost married him when I was seventeen. Pa wasn't much in favor of it. Then Harry decided he should marry within his tribe. He's a Coeur d'Alene. A finer man you won't find in all of Idaho whether he's white, black or Indian."

"Sound like you still like him."

"Yes, but he's married now. The city fathers wouldn't sell him the saddle shop so Pa bought it for him. It's still in my name since Indians can't own land or property in Idaho Territory."

"Seen that before. You have a shovel?"

"Oh, that. I figure no sense in telling the sheriff. He'll know about these two before we could get to him anyway. We'll bury them on the rise behind the house. I'm a good hand with a shovel."

She was. An hour later they had the two men in the ground. She saved all their personal goods to give to the sheriff. Put them in big envelopes and asked Buckskin to take them to town. She wrote the particulars of the men's death on the outside and signed both envelopes with the date.

Buckskin met the other two hands who were there. Two others were out on the range treating some minor ailments on two of the brood cows.

It had been early morning when he chanced on the attack on the ranch, now it was near noon and Mitzi fixed sandwiches and heated up some stew for them for dinner.

Soon he mounted up, took the envelopes and touched his hat brim.

"I'll be back tonight or tomorrow, depending on what I find out in the big city. I hope the waters are calm. In any event, I'll come back with some new glass for your windows. I measured the ones in the kitchen."

She smiled and the dimple popped in. "Buckskin, I don't know what to say. Been a long time since anyone has done something nice for me." She frowned. "You be careful in town."

On his way past the big barn, one of the hands waved at him and called him over. The man's name was Kent and Buckskin figured him to be a top cowhand.

"Going to town I hear," Kent said.

Buckskin nodded.

"Word will be out that somebody gunned two of the Lombard riders. Place will be as tense as a range war about ready to explode. Lombard is the law in Boise. He's got one triggerman called Slash Wade. He's a killer, pure and simple. Figured I better warn you to watch your back. Least I can do for saving the place from getting burned down. I got trapped in the barn without a rifle. Half the men in Boise will be looking for any stranger in town who can use a gun. Slash won't care if he kills two or three innocent men just so he gets the one who nailed the two Black Kettle riders."

Buckskin thanked him and headed down the ten mile wagon road to Boise. Now he was anxious to get to town and find out about his wanted poster, and to have a friendly talk with Slash Wade.

Buckskin started down the wagon road. As he remembered it, there had been no ranch between the Spade Bit and town twelve years ago. Now, evidently there was. Less than five miles down the wagon road he saw some ranch buildings ahead.

The structures had been put up well to the west of the road, where the Boise River ambled and twisted its way downgrade toward its merging with the mighty Snake River.

He was still half a mile away from the ranch buildings when a rider came away from them riding hard toward Buckskin. It wouldn't be a welcoming committee he was sure. They could have a lookout waiting for anyone coming from the Box R Ranch. There still was little in the way of settlement above the old Spade Bit.

It was too late to run and there was no place to hide, so Buckskin pulled the Spencer from his saddle boot, checked for a round in the chamber and settled down to a collision course with the hard charging rider.

The rider on a pure white mount was fifty yards away when Buckskin put a round over the mount's head with the Spencer. It brought an immediate reaction. The rider slammed to a stop, jerked a rifle from the boot, lifted it over his head and rode forward slowly.

Buckskin kept the rider under his sights all the way to where the mount stopped twenty yards away.

"Who the hell are you?" Buckskin bellowed.

The rifle came down slowly and the rider pushed it into leather, then urged the horse ahead gently with both his hands showing.

At ten yards Buckskin could see the rider was a young woman, hardly more than a girl. She came forward until he could see the worry lines around her eyes. She was pretty, young and angry.

"I'm no threat to you. I want to warn you. Pa sent two riders into town to find Slash. He's also got lookouts about a mile farther down the road. He figured somebody else must have been at the Box R Ranch to help them. Did you . . . did you kill the two men back there?"

"Yes, Miss. Anyone who attacks someone with a gun, must be ready to die at the hands of his enemies."

She nodded, her face working. "I don't like killing. It's so . . . so wasteful. Somehow I thought if I warned you that Slash was waiting, you might turn around and ride the other way. I don't know

17

you. Are you new to this area?"

"I lived here a lot of years ago."

"Oh. Then I guess you don't know what's going on. Pa is determined to get the Box R Ranch."

"Your father is the sheriff?"

She looked up and he caught the edge of a grin. Now he could see her soft green eyes, and long brown hair tumbling down from a low crowned tan hat with a string under her chin. She was slender and pretty and he bet her hair smelled like lilacs.

"Yes, Pa is sheriff. Don't mean a lot. I . . . I just wanted to warn you. There's another way to town."

"Thanks, I'll go that way. What does Slash Wade look like?"

"He's about as tall as you, dark hair. Wears all black usually. Has a three-inch scar on his cheek from a knife. That's why we call him Slash. He's a little heavier than you. He's not at all nice."

"If I see Slash, I'll give him your regards."

She shook her head. "Don't bother. You'll be busy enough. My Pa told Slash to find you and kill you."

Chapter Two

Buckskin Lee Morgan watched the brown haired ranch girl a moment and nodded. She was serious.

"A lot of men have tried to kill me. So far no one has succeeded. I'll watch for Slash. Does he have a favorite saloon in Boise?"

"The Bird Cage. They usually have a girl on a swing going back and forth. Oh, I'm Denise, Denise Lombard, but don't hold that last name against me." She paused and put on a glorious smile. "I do hope you don't get hurt in town. You're one of the best looking men I've seen in a long time."

He touched the brim of his hat. "Thanks, Miss, you're most kind. Also, I'll be watching for Slash."

He pulled his mount around and rode on down the trail toward Boise. A half mile farther on he turned sharply to the west, climbed a low wooded hill and went down the other side. The climb cut nearly two miles off the wagon road's journey to Boise and should outflank the lookouts the sheriff had sent out.

No use letting Slash know he was coming to town. The man presented a problem, but it was one that Buckskin had faced many times before. He'd play it as it came.

Just over an hour later, Buckskin tied his bay to a rail on a side street in Boise and found the saddle shop. This town had doubled in size since he'd seen it last. The leather goods store specialized in saddles and shoes, which made the operator an all around leather man.

Harry Blackhawk stood at a bench working on a saddle when Buckskin pushed open the screen door and stepped inside. The smell of newly tanned leather hit him like a fond memory. Something about the scent of leather stirred him and brought back the old days when Barney used to work on a saddle in the small barn at the Spade Bit.

The man turned when the door closed and waved. "Just a minute and I'll be with you. Got to pull a few stitches tight before they weld themselves to the leather."

"Go right ahead working," Buckskin said. "I came mostly to talk. Mitzi Roland said I could trust you."

Harry grinned. "Sweet Mitzi, nice lady. I hear she's having some problems with running the ranch. Wish to hell that no-good brother of hers could be some help."

"Met him, couldn't figure him out."

Harry snorted. "Yeah, that's the way he affects

most folks. He's not slow-witted, nothing like that. He's just spineless, no good, lazy, and smart enough to know how to play dumb."

"Doesn't sound like much help for Mitzi."

Harry turned and stared at Buckskin. Harry was all Indian, black hair he had cut short, broad face, heavy nose, black eyes, a square jaw and almost no whiskers. It was a strong, honest face. Buckskin grinned as the Indian took stock of the white man.

"Do I pass inspection?"

"Damn near. Tied down gun failed you. Why the fast draw rig?"

"I need it from time to time."

Harry nodded and went back to the saddle he was working on. He was lacing the final covering on the horn with leather thongs to hold the cap in place.

"Why were you talking with Mitzi?"

"Just happened by. How long you been in town?"

"Come July it'll be eight years."

"Ever hear of the Spade Bit Horse Ranch?"

"Yep. It was a good one. Not around anymore."

"I grew up there. My dad was Frank Leslie. He ran it for years."

Harry stopped and grinned. "I knew Frank. I was just a kid at the time. Our tribe used to bring him horses now and then. Good man."

"I went back to take a look at the old home place. While I looked at the ranch house, ten riders stormed into the yard shooting up a storm."

"That'd be raiders from the Black Kettle. I warned Mitzi that they were getting bolder. Damn Sheriff Lombard thinks he owns the whole county."

"From what I've heard, he just about does. I've got another small problem I want your help on."

"You fixing to lend a hand to Mitzi, as well?"

"The idea had crossed my mind. I don't like to see a big outfit take advantage of a small lady that way."

"Good, we'll talk about it. Now, what's that other problem you have?"

Five minutes later, Buckskin had told Harry all about the spurious wanted poster there in Boise twelve years ago and how it came about. Harry nodded and tightened the one piece of leather that formed the cantle and the seat of the saddle and pulled it tight down both sides.

"I can check the drawer full of wanted posters over at the sheriff's office," Harry said. "I do some tracking for them from time to time. I'll go over there right now and see what I can find." The Indian hesitated. "Have you heard about Slash Wade yet?"

Buckskin eased the Colt .45 an inch in and out of the holster. "Heard about him a dozen times— three, actually. Is he what his rep makes him out to be?"

"I've never seen him draw, but I've heard he's fast. Do know that he's ruthless, has all the morals of a rattlesnake and would rather shoot a man in the back than give him a chance. If you tangled with the Black Kettle riders, Sheriff Lombard will have sicced Slash on your trail yesterday."

"So I've heard. He's my next stop, just as soon as I find out if any of that old paper on me is still floating around. I'd just as soon not get thrown into jail on that manufactured charge."

Harry put down his awl, took off a leather apron and hung it on the saddle horn. "I'll get over there right now and see what I can find. I look through the wanteds every now and then. They won't think it unusual."

Harry grinned. "Now you're wondering where I learned to speak English but too polite to ask. No problem. I was one of those Indian brats who got lost from his band after a fight with the cavalry and picked up by a friendly rancher. He never could find my parents. He tried a dozen times. In the end he gave up and raised me as his own. Sent me through nine grades and then decided that was enough.

"I was a cowboy on his ranch for five more years, but loved working leather. When he died and his widow sold out, I came to town and hung around the leather shop until the elderly owner let me learn the trade from him. He died about five years ago and Mitzi's father bought the place and hired me to run it. A year later he gave me the store but kept it in his name . . . you know."

Buckskin held out his hand. "Good to meet you, Harry. I'll get a cup of coffee and see what I can learn about the town. She's grown one hell of a lot since I used to live here."

Almost an hour later, Buckskin had finished two cups of coffee and a piece of cherry pie, when he saw Harry Blackhawk open his saddle and shoe shop. Buckskin paid his tab and strolled over to the leather store.

Harry grinned. "Didn't find a blessed thing on you in the drawer of posters over there. Not a trace. I found one wanted that was seven years old. I showed it to a deputy and asked him how long they kept paper like that. He said not this long. He tore it up and threw it away. That's probably happened with anything twelve years old in that drawer."

Buckskin nodded. "Good. Now I can breathe a little easier. Where is that saloon where Slash Wade hangs out?"

"You're going to face him down in his home den? I guess that figures. The Bird Cage Saloon is his favorite drinking hole. It's down half a block on the other side of the street." He went back to the saddle and measured the stirrup leather against the fender.

Harry looked up, concern on his face. "Don't know how much you're going to get involved in this affair. But you should know that Sheriff Lombard has a son, Gage, who is crazy over Mitzi. Claims he's going to marry her and has warned everyone else to stay away from her. He's wild, drinks a lot, is a deputy sheriff, and almost as much of a worthless skunk as Mitzi's brother. Watch out for him."

"Thanks, I guess I'm involved. Mitzi offered me the job of ramrod on her ranch."

Buckskin touched the brim of his hat and walked out letting the screen door close gently as he eyed the Bird Cage Saloon down the street.

It was just after four in the afternoon when Buckskin finished his beer at the Bird Cage. The velvet swing was not being used. The whores working the afternoon drinking crowd were not the best of the crop that year, and he had checked out every man in the place but Slash Wade was not among them. Buckskin stopped by to see Harry

Blackhawk on the way back to his horse.

"Didn't find Slash, so both of us are still alive," Buckskin said.

Blackhawk looked up and pulled a thread tight on the saddle. "You help take care of that lady. She's had a rough start in life so far. Should be some way to smooth things out a bit. Going out there you keep one hand on your Colt and one hand on your hair."

Buckskin grinned. He'd never heard an Indian use that old saying. The hand on your hair was to keep you from being scalped. Blackhawk chuckled, then broke into a belly laugh as Buckskin went out and closed the door.

He rode the shortcut back to the ranch and was almost at the end of the downgrade when he saw a horse in a fringe of woods to his left. A moment later the horse and a rider came out and rode toward him.

At once he saw that the rider was Denise, the girl from the Black Kettle Ranch who had warned him about Slash Wade. He slowed and she came up and rode beside him, so close her leg touched his.

"You in any big hurry?" she asked. "I see Slash didn't hurt you."

Buckskin stopped his mount and she did as well still beside him.

"A hurry? Not especially."

"Good, come over here, I have something to show you." She turned her horse away from him and rode back into the brush and woods thirty yards away. They both entered the woods and were soon out of sight of the trail. They came to a small stream with a blush of new green grass on the near bank. She slipped down from her horse.

Denise looked at him with a small frown. "Well come on, silly. I can't show you from here. I'm Denise, just in case you've forgotten. You never did tell me your name."

He stepped down from his bay, let the reins fall to the ground to keep the mount close by and nodded. "Oh, yes, Denise, I remember your name. I'm Buckskin Lee Morgan."

"Buckskin," she said as if thinking about the name. "Yes, I like it. Right down this way."

They went along the narrow stream for fifty feet, then came to a blanket on the grass with two pillows and a bottle of wine.

"I thought we might have a little party so I could welcome you properly back to Boise."

She stepped close to him, reached up and kissed him firmly on the lips, then put her arms around him and pushed her soft body hard against his.

"I so hope that you aren't in any hurry to get back to the ranch."

He caught her shoulders and pushed her away a moment. Then he bent and kissed her hard on her mouth feeling it open and stabbed his tongue deep into her as she circled his torso with her arms and pressed her hips solidly against his. He could feel the sudden sexual heat from her body radiating into him. It gave him a jolt and his pulse quickened.

When the kiss ended she smiled, caught his hand and led him to the blanket.

"No one will see us here. Hardly anyone uses the shortcut anymore and if they do, we're so hidden they couldn't find us unless we fired off a canon."

They sat on the blanket and she caught at his shirt, opening the buttons down to his leather vest, stripping that off him and then putting her hands inside his shirt on his hairy chest.

"Oh, yes. I like a man with hair on his chest." She took his hand and put it on her breasts. They had been hidden behind a loose blouse. He worked open two buttons and pressed inside the cloth to find she wore nothing under the outer garment.

His hand closed on one breast and she gasped, then smiled and nodded.

"Oh, yes, I love that. I die for the way I feel when I'm touched and petted there. I love it."

She put one hand to his fly and touched the growing bulge. "I think you like me," she said, then gasped again when he changed breasts with his hand under her white blouse. "Oh, damn but that feels good."

He took his hand away and opened the rest of the buttons on her blouse. He pushed back the cloth to reveal both her breasts. They showed larger than he figured, with small pink areolas and nipples still pinker and beginning to bloom with hot blood. Buckskin bent and kissed one breast, and then the other.

She sat tall, pushing her chest out for his ministrations. He kept at them, kissing them again, licking them from base to top, then licking her nipples until she whimpered. Her breathing quickened. Her sexual heat grew and grew and he felt it coming from every pore in her body. He topped his work on her breasts by sucking half of one big breast into his mouth and chewing tenderly on her soft flesh.

"Oh, God!" she shouted. She pulled him with her as she bent backwards on the blanket. He draped half over her still fastened to her breast. She moaned and whimpered, then her knees lifted and spread and her hips began to pound upward as a slashing climax tore through her slender body.

"Oh, yes, oh yes! So good, so good. Mmm. Yes, yes, yes, yes." Then she couldn't talk anymore and her voice came in a long, high wail as her hips pounded against him again and again.

For a moment she was quiet; then the tremors hit her again and shook her body like a mountain lion with a rabbit in its mouth. Sweat beaded her forehead and her mouth opened to gasp and suck in all the air she could.

She panted for breath, wailing at the same time. Her hands both moved to his fly and she tore at the buttons.

Then as suddenly as it began, it ended. She slumped back to the blanket, let her knees fall and close and her arms came around his shoulders again, pinning his mouth to her breast as she would a newborn.

"Oh damn," she said softly. "I usual don't pop that way before I get your big long stick rammed into my little cunnie. Lordy, what a ride that was. Lordy, but that was fine. That good and we're just getting started."

She sat up and pushed Buckskin down on his back. Slowly she undid the buttons on his pants fly and opened them. Then she slid down his underwear and squealed when his erection popped out hard and pulsating. She bent and kissed

28

the purple head of him, then kissed his lips.

"I don't do mouth suckoff for you," she said softly. "Not yet. Maybe when I'm older."

She pulled off his boots, then his pants and the short underwear and sat on her feet watching him. She had shucked out of her blouse and Buckskin enjoyed watching her big breasts bounce and sway as she worked undressing him. When he was naked she lay down on top of him and giggled.

"I'm going to keep my skirt on, but I'll take off my bloomers. I don't like to get all bare out in the woods this way. Somebody might sneak up on us." She giggled. "But don't worry. Nobody knows we're here. Nobody saw us come in here. We're safe."

She lifted her hips from him and worked her bloomers down off her hips and kicked them off, then lay down on him again, her warm crotch smothering his erection.

"Oh, yes, now that is nice," Denise said. She began to rotate her hips on him and Buckskin yelped in wonder at how strongly it aroused him.

"Have you ever been on top?" he asked.

"Me, on top of you and . . . and doing it?"

"Yes. I'd bet you haven't."

He pushed apart her legs and lifted her away from him. She caught his long rod and guided it and Buckskin moaned as it penetrated the wet, slippery slot.

"Oh, damn!" Denise said. She lowered herself slowly, then in a frenzy, dropped all the way down and shrilled a lilting scream as his penis drove into her the full distance.

"Oh, Lordy, that feels wonderful but different. You're touching something inside me that ain't never been touched that way before. Lordy, but that is marvelous."

"Lift up and then let yourself down," Buckskin said.

"Really? I have to do the work?"

"You have me pinned to the blanket," Buckskin said.

She lifted tentatively, then went down. She grinned. Again she did the movement and then she went higher and with each drop she brayed in wonder. At last she set up a rhythm that he could respond to and then with each drop he pistoned his hips upward to meet her dropping body.

"Oh, my God! I've never felt anything like that." She nodded and her face turned serious as she concentrated on the movements. Buckskin stood it as long as he could, then he caught hold of her and rolled over putting her on the bottom. He caught her legs and lifted them straight up, then let them down on his shoulders.

This changed his entry position. He shifted higher, then began to thrust quickly into her with short, sharp strokes that brought him to the point of explosion in a short time.

"You about ready?" she asked looking up at him with awe.

He nodded. Then the whole world blasted apart in his face and the heavens tilted and the planets flew off their orbits and the solar system crashed with everything falling back into the sun, which produced a white-hot burning light that blinded him for a moment. Then he could see plainly and there was nothing but white on white.

"Hey, you okay?"

He frowned. The voice sounded human.

"I didn't kill you, did I?"

Buckskin grinned. He opened his eyes and pulled her legs down and took another long, deep breath to try to replenish his oxygen starved body.

"Oh, yes, but I think you did kill me there for just a few minutes. I exploded all over the place."

"I know that. You near shot all the way through me."

They lay side by side staring at the canopy of green leaves over them and listened to the chattering of the water as it headed downhill over the pebbles and rocks of the tiny stream.

"You have a wonderful way to welcome a man into the community," Buckskin said.

She laughed. "Oh, I don't do this that often. You were so damn good looking and I figured you'd be coming back, so I got this ready just in case. Not many handsome men come out this way, and Pa keeps a tight rein on me usually. Today he went to town with Slash to try to find out who gunned down his two men."

"Maybe I can meet them later."

"Oh, God, I hope not. I want to do this again, lots of times. I ain't never had me a man like you before. Only diddled around a bit with two boys who were just learning. It was their first time but they wouldn't admit it. I had to show them what to do. They could do it all right. One of them shot off five times in two hours. But he didn't even think about me, about my wanting to do it too."

Buckskin sat up and reached for his underwear.

"No, don't leave yet. Let's do it again."

"Nothing I'd like better, but I need to get on up to the Box R. They're expecting me."

She sat up and went to her knees in front of him and pushed one big breast up to his mouth. "Chew on me again. That makes me go wild."

He kissed her breast, then the other one and eased her away. "Next get together we'll have more time. We'll explore and experiment and I'll show you some new ways to make love. Maybe we can play all afternoon, maybe all night. Have you ever spent all night with a man before?"

"No, but I'd like to with you."

"We'll see."

He pulled on his pants and his boots. She dressed as well and a few minutes later they walked back to their horses. She pushed up and kissed him one last time, then grinned and stepped into her saddle astride. "I will see you again, make love to you again. I'll arrange it. I have ways. Now get your big frame out of here and up the trail. I'll go out another way so no one could even suspect."

Buckskin touched his hat and rode.

It took him almost an hour to finish his ride to the Box R Ranch. He found Mitzi Roland pacing the screened-in porch. When she saw him coming just before dusk, she ran out to meet him.

"Thank God, you've come. One of the hands said he saw six riders not two hours ago rustling our herd of a hundred market-ready steers and heading them toward the Lombard Black Kettle range. What on earth are we going to do?"

Chapter Three

"Mr. Morgan," Mitzi shouted. "What are we going to do about the rustlers?"

Buckskin Lee Morgan stepped down from his bay and took his low crowned hat off and reset it. Then he looked at the owner of the Box R Ranch.

"We're going after them, Miss Roland. How many rifles do you have on the place?"

Twenty minutes later, Buckskin and the four Box R hands left the ranch riding hard for the spot where the one-hundred head of prime steers were last seen. It was dark by the time they got there. Buckskin had brought along two lanterns and he lit one and identified the trail.

"No way to hide four-hundred hoofprints," he said to one of the hands. "Now all we have to do is follow the trail and see where our friends took the beef. Then we take them back."

"Somebody could get hurt doing this," the cowhand said. He was called Toby. Then he grinned. "Hell, I'm game. Most exciting thing that's happened to me since I left Cincinnati three years ago."

The trail led generally south. Every quarter mile, Buckskin stopped the crew and lit the lantern and checked for the trail. It was still there. They could almost follow it in the pale moonlight of a half orb, but needed to check.

"Heading for the Black Kettle Ranch sure as hell," another cowhand said. "Looks like we're not going anywhere near the ranch buildings. Probably to some canyon or valley up against the hills."

They tracked the animals for an hour. By that time they were well inside the Black Kettle range. The moon came out brighter as some small clouds scudded away and Buckskin could track the herd easily by the night light.

"What we do when we find them?" the hand Buckskin remembered was called Jody asked.

"We take them back, drive them to their home range. Then, if there's time, we pay a small visit to the Black Kettle's biggest barn."

"Oh, boy," Jody said. "What we do at the barn?"

"You'll have to wait and see, Jody."

Another half hour and they saw a the hint of a fire ahead. Smoke came toward them and Buckskin swore. "Branding fire," he said. "This bunch ain't wasting any time. Anybody here ever shot a man before?"

One older hand grunted. "Got me a few Rebs at the end of the big war."

"No different here," Buckskin said. "These men

are rustlers, and the penalty for that in this territory is hanging. A bullet works just as well. If they put up a fight, we fight back, understood?" Buckskin looked around and saw heads nod in the darkness.

"How many men did they have when they took the herd?" Buckskin asked.

"Five of them I could see," a voice said from the darkness. "Might have been one more."

"We've got five. Not bad odds."

They came closer to the fire, and Buckskin could see two mounted men bringing in steers and throwing them. He stopped about fifty yards from the fire. He sent three men to circle a quarter of the way around the fire and told them not to shoot until they heard two rounds. The first one would be his.

"If they fire back, then we cut them down. Doubt that they'll put up a fight being in the firelight and us in the dark. But you never can tell. We don't care if the two mounted men ride off."

Five minutes later, Buckskin figured the men were in place. He ground tied his mount, took his Spencer and two extra tubes of rounds and sat down on the valley grass. With his elbows on his knees for bracing, he took careful aim at the man closest to the fire. The man had just picked up a red hot branding iron when Buckskin squeezed the trigger.

The big .52 caliber slug couldn't miss. It pounded into and through the cowboy's right thigh, spinning him around, bringing a scream of pain as he jolted backward into the dust and dirt.

When the sound of the rifle shot echoed away

into the hills, Buckskin used his parade ground voice and bellowed out a warning.

"You're surrounded. You're charged with rustling beef from the Box R. Put your six-guns on the ground and lift your hands, or you're dead where you stand."

Two men near the fire obeyed at once. A third close to the shadows dove out of the light and to safety. Buckskin heard the two riders' horses pound away into the deeper darkness.

"Move in," Buckskin shouted and he and the man he was with trotted up to the fire, their rifles covering the two men there. One brayed in pain from his shot leg.

Buckskin gathered up the men's revolvers and rifles, caught the three horses and threw dirt on the fire not wanting to make himself an easy target from the darkness.

He had one of the men tie up the leg wound on the shot rustler.

"Wouldn't want you to bleed to death and cheat the hangman out of his fee," Buckskin said.

Ten minutes later they had the herd of unhappy steers up from their lay-down and moving back toward the Box R range. The two rustlers had been tied on their horses and the youngest of the Box R riders given the job of leading them back to the ranch.

It had been half a dozen years since Buckskin had done any cattle driving. He found it just as dirty and hard as it had been then, only now twice the pain since it was dark.

Once the herd got moving they kept them at a good pace. Buckskin figured three miles an hour would be the hoped for rate.

It was well past three o'clock in the morning by the star clock when Buckskin called a halt. They were well inside the Box R range by that time. He left one man to ride shotgun on the herd, and sent the other two back to the ranch house where he told them to tie up the two rustlers. They would take them to town in the morning and charge them with rustling with the Idaho Territorial Attorney General.

"What about me?" Jody asked.

"You and me are going visiting," Buckskin said. "You still have that second lantern?"

Jody grinned in the moonlight. "Damn right and I know what to do with it."

It was almost four-thirty when the two riders came in sight of the Black Kettle Ranch. They left their horses tied a quarter of a mile away and slipped up on the backside of the big barn. It was three stories tall, built to hold many tons of cut hay to use when the stock was belly deep in winter snow.

Buckskin moved cautiously, expecting a lookout. He didn't see or hear anyone, and walked the last twenty feet to the back of the barn as if he belonged there. He held the unlit lantern beside his leg. Jody was doing the same thing at the other end of the barn.

They each found small doors in the ends of the barn and slipped inside. Buckskin saw the ideal spot to start the fire and emptied the lantern of its coal oil onto a pile of hay that reached to a six-foot square hole in the second floor that led to the haymow above.

He struck his match and tossed it into the coal oil. A little had vaporized and it whooshed into flames. In five minutes no one would be able to put out the fire.

Buckskin slipped out of the back door and ran into the darkness. He heard someone just down from him and soon saw Jody pounding along toward their horses. They mounted and watched the growing flames squirt out a window and then a first floor door.

A banging dinner bell sounded from the ranch house and moments later lights danced in the windows as men rushed outside toward the barn. Buckskin and Jody turned their mounts and walked them away from the pyre. Once when Buckskin looked back, he saw the flames break through the roof.

"Let's get on back to the ranch," Buckskin said.

Jody laughed. "Oh, yeah. I wonder what old Sheriff Lombard will have to say about this. When we complained to him about somebody burning down our barn, he said the cause was spontaneous combustion from green hay we'd cut. Yeah, another case of spontaneous combustion only this time it's in his own barn."

It was daylight when the two riders returned their horses to the Box R Ranch corral. They both stumbled into the bunkhouse and fell asleep as soon as they hit the blankets.

The other men awoke the two at noon for dinner.

They all ate around a big table in the ranch house kitchen. Mitzi did the cooking and was proud of her table. She speared a baked potato and looked at Buckskin.

"You said we were going to take our two rustlers into town today?"

Buckskin nodded. "Figured. Guess I'm slept out. We better keep one man with a rifle guarding those steers until we can drive them to the stock yards. Pick a man. I want Jody and one other man with me to take the rustlers in. Might be best if you could come along with us, Miss Roland."

"I'll be ready to leave at one-thirty."

"Buggy?"

"No, I'll ride. How do we get around the Black Kettle? They'll probably have guards out looking for us?"

"Take the short cut over Green Mountain. If we have to, we'll shoot our way through. We'll all be armed with rifles and six-guns. Doubt if the sheriff will bother us. He'll figure we'll take the rustlers to his office. On that one we fool him."

"Can the Territorial Attorney General bring charges?" Mitzi asked.

"Absolutely. We'll swear that the sheriff is prejudiced in this case and is the defendant-in-fact and the Attorney General will be bound by law to place the charges. He still might send the culprits to the county jail, but they'll be under his control."

Mitzi nodded. "Sounds good, if it works. I've been trying to figure out a way to go around the sheriff for a year now."

An hour and a half later, the four from the Box R herded the two rustlers on their own horses along the trail over Green Mountain. Not a man stood in their way or fired at them from ambush.

When they came up behind the territorial capitol building, Buckskin told them to wait while he found out where to go. He was back soon and he and Mitzi led the two culprits into the Attorney General's office on the second floor.

It took them two stern talks to get past a male secretary and an assistant before they were shown into the Attorney General's office.

Buckskin spelled out the charges and the territory's head lawman scowled.

"I've heard bad things about Sheriff Lombard before, but nothing with this kind of bite to it."

"I'm charging Isaiah Lombard and these two men with rustling, Mr. Perkins," Mitzi said.

"Miss Roland, that's a capital offense. These men could be hanged. Is that what you want?"

"I want them charged and tried. If they hang or not is up to the judge and jury. I want Isaiah Lombard treated like any other common criminal."

"You have proof?"

Buckskin spoke up. "Yes, sir. We have an eyewitness who saw six riders from the Black Kettle Ranch drive the herd of a hundred market-ready steers off the Box R range. I and four of our hands tracked the steers off the Box R range, into the Black Kettle lands. There we surprised these two men and four others blanking out the Box R brand and reburning the steers with the B-K brand.

"We surrounded them and I fired once wounding this man. He and another in the firelight gave up. The other four fled. We have the blanking and rebranding irons, two perpetrators, and more than a dozen steers with the fresh brands on them. These men were rustling on specific orders from the Black Kettle Ranch owner, Isaiah Lombard, and we're charging him with rustling as well."

"I'm not the judge here, Mr. Morgan. But you have plenty of evidence to file the complaint. I'll have my clerk write it up at once."

"Will you also issue arrest warrants for the three men so named?" Buckskin asked.

"Afraid so. Lombard is going to be furious."

"We ask that he be incarcerated until the trial date along with these two," Buckskin said.

"Well, that will be up to the judge. I'll personally pick up Lombard and bring him before the district court judge tomorrow for arraignment. After that, it's up to the district attorney."

"Your office won't be prosecuting?"

"Not unless it's a territorial wide case. We'll send this to the district for trial."

"My guess is that Sheriff Lombard will twist the district attorney around his sheriff's badge. He'll probably never even stand trial."

"If not, then you're free to charge malfeasance under color of authority, and we'll have a territorial charge."

Mitzi stamped her foot. "I knew this sounded too easy. Well, Mr. Perkins, we're waiting. Have those charges filed right now and we'll sign them. I want to go along when you arrest Sheriff Lombard and put him in the territorial lockup."

Perkins wiped his forehead with a linen handkerchief. "Small problem there, Miss Roland. We don't yet have a territorial prison. We use the facilities in various counties."

"So Lombard would be housed in his own jail?" Mitzi asked, her brown eyes flashing.

"I'm afraid so. Best we can do right now. I'm on your side in this, but unseating an elected sheriff

41

is hard. Much harder when he has the power that Sheriff Lombard has."

"At least we can try," Buckskin said.

The Territorial Attorney General looked at a wall clock. "I'm afraid we can't do much more today. It's nearly four-thirty."

"No," Mitzi shouted. "I demand that you write those complaints and arrest and jail the three men involved right now. I don't care if you have to work an hour or so overtime."

Perkins lifted his brows and sighed. "Yes, Miss Roland. I'll get right on it."

"Good, we'll wait, and we'll watch."

Fifteen minutes later Territorial Attorney General Floyd Perkins led the small parade down the street to the county office building and the sheriff's office. They went in and a deputy came to the small counter across the front of the room.

"Yes sir?"

"Is Sheriff Lombard here," Perkins asked.

"Yes sir, but he's busy at the moment."

"I'm afraid whatever he's doing will have to wait. I have a warrant for his arrest." Perkins waved the folded paper at the deputy, pushed through the hinged doors and headed for the sheriff's private office that had the door closed.

Buckskin was right behind him. The deputy stood there watching them with his mouth open. Perkins opened the door and scowled. The room was empty.

He spun to face the deputy.

"I . . . I guess he had to go out. He has a rear door."

"I'll post a man here to wait for him," Perkins snapped. "In the meantime, I have two territorial prisoners for you to jail. Remember the rules on territorial prisoners. If any harm comes to them, or if they escape, each man here will be charged. Do I make myself clear?"

"Yes, sir, Territorial Attorney General Perkins. We understand. You have the papers?"

Five minutes later the two men were jailed and the doctor was sent for to treat the shot up leg.

Outside the courthouse, Buckskin and the other three from the Box R talked a moment.

Mitzi motioned to the two riders. "Take the night off and do the town," she said. "You two have any of your wages left?"

They both nodded.

"You be back to work come sunup. We have a lot to do around that place yet."

When they left, Buckskin turned to his employer. "Hungry, Miss Roland? I'd like to take you out to supper for a change so you don't have to do the cooking."

Her frown had begun to weaken. His suggestion finished it off and soft touches of a smile worked around the edges of her pretty face.

"Yes, Mr. Morgan. I'd like that. There is one restaurant here that isn't terrible. But I insist on paying."

He touched her arm. "Not a chance. When I ask a pretty lady out to supper, I'm the one who pays."

She lifted her brows and stared at him a moment. Then she smiled and nodded. "I'd be honored to be your guest."

At the restaurant, they ordered and then Mitzi looked at Buckskin with a frown.

"I'm worried that Sheriff Lombard will never be arrested on that warrant. As fast as we got over there today, somehow Lombard knew we were coming. He has eyes and ears everywhere. He knew you and I were in town and that we had his two men. He knew everything, so he simply vanished when we came with the warrant."

"If he did all that so fast, he's good," Buckskin said. "I'm tying to figure his next move. His rustling didn't work, he escaped from the hanging charge, what's next for him?"

Mitzi looked up and anger and fear bathed her face. "Not hard to guess. None of this happened until you came to town. He's out hunting you, right now, him and Slash Wade." Her eyes flared in fear. "We shouldn't be here. We should forget the supper and get out of town."

Buckskin put his hand on the woman's hand. "No," he said softly. "I don't run from any man. Let them come, maybe we can settle a few things quickly and you can get back to running your ranch."

"You don't understand. This is Slash Wade we're talking about. He lives by the rattlesnake code. Strike first without warning, strike again and again as long as your target is standing. Never give your enemies an even chance. Shoot them in the back if at all possible."

Buckskin smiled. "Look at me. I'm sitting with my back to the wall. I have a perfect view of everyone coming into the room. My right hand is free and you're slightly off center of our table to give me a clear shot at the door. If you want references, I can give you a dozen names, but you'd have to go to a bunch of cemeteries to find them. Now relax and enjoy your supper."

Their food came and the waiter hovered. He

smiled at them and then spoke to Mitzi. "Miss Roland, it's good to see you here again. I remember when you and your father used to come every Sunday for dinner."

"Thank you, Roger. One of these days I'll get back to church and to having dinner here. Right now we're too busy. Oh, this is my new foreman at the ranch."

"Good to have you both with us," Roger said and backed away.

Buckskin's forehead showed lines of concern. "Mitzi, why didn't you tell him my name?"

"Because he's one of the Sheriff's spies. Right now he's on his way to the sheriff's office to report that you and I are having supper here. I knew this was a bad idea."

Buckskin checked the room. There were about twenty tables. Half of them were full. No one was being turned away at the door.

"You may be right. But if you are, nothing will happen in here. They would gradually clear the room if they were moving in on us here."

"The back door?" Mitzi asked.

Buckskin chuckled. "Do that and spoil their fun? If they're out there, they expect us to come out together, and not too long from now. We will, only you'll get away to one side quickly while I do a little fast moving in the other direction. If we split up, our horses are still behind the territorial capitol building. We'll meet there."

She caught his hand, the food forgotten on their plates. "You do expect trouble, don't you?"

"Yes. The man moves like an Apache war party across an open plain and you never see them. How much daylight do we have left?"

"This time of year it gets dark about seven o'clock."

He checked his pocket Waterbury. "We still have more than an hour. I'd just as soon do it in the daylight." He stood. "You need to come out with me so they'll know who to shoot."

She looked up at him with terror in her eyes. Her face quivered, eyes wide and her chin trembled.

He touched her chin. "Easy. Just an expression. But we hit the front door and you move at once to your left away from me. I'll be on your right. Understand?"

She nodded, her face still a glaze of fear.

"Might as well do it now. Neither one of us is going to finish eating our supper."

He stood, held her chair and moved it back, then let her take his arm. He stopped at a small cash counter and paid the bill, then headed for the door.

"Oh, Mr. Morgan, you forgot your change," the cashier said.

Buckskin turned back to the counter without Mitzi. He ignored the dollar bill and coins and grabbed the cashier by the shirt front and jerked him off his feet so he bellied up over the small table.

"How did you know my name?"

"Why the waiter told me. Yes, the waiter."

Buckskin could see the fear in the man's eyes.

"He didn't know it either. I just hope to hell your spying for Lombard is going to be worth it. I think I'll take you out front with me."

The cashier's face went flat white, his eyes rolled up and he shook like a leaf in a windstorm.

46

"No sir, I wouldn't like that. Don't want to do that, Mr. Morgan, no sir."

"Why not? You deserve some time in the fresh air outside."

Buckskin pulled him from behind the counter and prodded him in front of himself as he nodded at Mitzi. They walked toward the door.

"Cashier man, with any luck you should live ten or fifteen seconds after we get through your front door."

The cashier let out a small cry and crumpled to the floor.

"Fainted," Buckskin said. He drew his six-gun from leather and looked at Mitzi. "Remember, as soon as we're out the door, you turn and run to your left, fast."

She nodded.

Buckskin put his hand on the front door, turned the knob and rammed it outward hard.

Chapter Four

Buckskin Lee Morgan went through the front door of the restaurant fast and in front of Mitzi. He saw no lineup of men in the street or to the left and charged to his right. The first shot came from across the street out of the hardware store's front door. It sounded like a rifle but the shooter led him too much and the round smashed the window of a real estate firm behind Buckskin.

Buckskin heard a pair of handguns blasting away and he dove to the boardwalk. He came up behind a pair of fifty-gallon wooden barrels outside the hardware store.

He spotted puffs of smoke from across the street more than fifty feet away. Not good range for a hogleg, difficult but not impossible. The rifle spoke again, the bullet splintering a shower of wood shards off the edge of the barrel. The lead and wood slivers missed him.

He saw the rifleman standing in the open across the way levering in a new round. Taking careful aim, Buckskin pushed out the Colt and leaned around the wooden barrel. He fired three times as fast as he could, lifting each shot a little higher.

The first round hit the rifleman in the right leg, the second one caught him in the gut and before he moved, the third heavy lead slug slammed through his forehead dumping him backward against a women's wear store window where he bounced off the frame and sprawled in death on the boardwalk.

A half dozen more shots came from the pistolmen, but they were firing from hiding in the shadows under the overhang and from doorways. Buckskin watched from behind the barrel another minute. Nobody else fired at him. Neither did anyone come out to the boardwalk from that section of the street.

A tin whistle shrilled down the street. Buckskin looked that way. A young man wearing a fancy embroidered fringed shirt, high crown white hat and wearing twin, pearl handled six-guns came marching up the street shrilling the whistle every ten feet. When he approached the scene of the shootout, he dropped the whistle from his mouth and let it hang on a cord around his neck.

"Cease fire, damnit. I'm County Deputy Sheriff Gage Lombard. Who the hell is shooting up the street? It's illegal to discharge a firearm in the city limits of Boise. Who the hell was shooting?"

Buckskin stood slowly and when he received no more fire, he slid his six-gun back in leather.

"You better ask the four bushwhackers who shot at me when I came out of the restaurant a

Kit Dalton

few minutes ago," Buckskin barked at the man. The deputy turned his way and walked over. He was young, no more than twenty, Buckskin figured. His flashy clothes were matched by a handlebar moustache that curled two-inches on each side of his face, good length for a kid so young. Otherwise he was clean shaven, slender and looked well muscled.

"Who are you, loudmouth?" the deputy challenged.

"I'm the target who four bushwhackers just used for gunnery practice. Why aren't you out looking for them?"

"Didn't see nothing illegal. Just heard the shots."

"Check the hombre over there by the women's wear store. He was the one with a rifle, but he won't shoot it no more."

"You killed him? From this side of the street with a six-gun?"

"Peers that way, don't it. You see any rifle I'm packing?"

"Don't go smart mouth with me, gunslick, or I'll have you in a jail cell so fast your trigger finger will be twitching without a hogleg."

Mitzi hurried up beside Buckskin and took his arm.

"Gage, everything Mr. Morgan said is true. He's my new foreman at the ranch. We were having supper and when we came out, four men started shooting at Mr. Morgan. I saw them. One of them was Penn Sawyer. He shot three times at Mr. Morgan. I want you to arrest Penn."

As soon as the deputy saw Mitzi, his attitude changed. The snarl left his voice, his face relaxed and smiled. He walked toward her and grinned.

"Mitzi. Good to see you. I still want to take you to the barn dance down at the big feed store Saturday night. You never answered my letter."

"Can't go, Gage. Now what you gonna do about the men who tried to gun down my foreman?"

"Oh, well, I don't know. Let's take a look at the rifleman."

The three walked across the street and pushed back a crowd of ten people who had gathered around the dead man.

"Stranger," Gage said. "I don't know him." He looked at the crowd. "Any of you recognize this man?"

Nobody said anything. One man started to say something, then shook his head.

Then a cowboy nodded. "Yep, I saw him last night down at the Bird Cage Saloon. He was pretty well drunk. Wasn't bothering anybody, just drinking a little."

Gage looked at the body. "Three hits, from across the street? You some kind of a marksman or something? That's damn near fifty, fifty-five feet across there." He shook his head. "Damn fine shooting under fire." He looked up at Buckskin. "You say he shot first?"

"Yes, check the magazine on the repeater. I guarantee you it won't be full."

The deputy picked up the dropped rifle and pumped three rounds out of the magazine.

"That's a Remington-Keene repeating rifle and it holds seven rounds," Buckskin said. "He fired three times and missed me. Satisfied?"

"For now. I'll make out a report." He motioned to two men near by. "Get this body down to the undertaker. Maybe he can figure out who he is."

Gage Lombard moved up closer to Buckskin and spoke softly. "I better warn you, sport. Mitzi is my girl. We're promised. She's going to be my wife."

Mitzi swung her hand out sharply and slapped Gage on the face. She sputtered for a minute then screamed at him. "No such thing. I wouldn't marry you if you was the last man in Idaho territory. No such thing. What's more, I hate you Gage Lombard. I hate you!"

She caught Buckskin's arm and turned him and they walked away. Her face had stained red and she huffed as she breathed. She took one more look over her shoulder and shook her head in fury.

"I can't discourage him. I don't know what to say to him. He keeps telling people we're promised. Not a bit of truth to it."

Buckskin grinned. "I believe you. He's the sheriff's son?"

"He is, and as bad as his father. One of the men who shot at you is his best friend. I think Penn Sawyer really works for the sheriff doing his dirty jobs, like killing people."

She looked over her shoulder and then urged him ahead faster.

"What's he doing back there?"

"Staring at us like he wished he could grab one of his guns and shoot you down so he wouldn't have to worry about you." She pulled his arm tighter against her body until it touched the side of her breast.

"He just hates to see me with a man, any other man. I've never encouraged him at all. I used to go to school with his sister, Denise, but I never even looked at him. He's not the kind of a man I like." Mitzi grinned and looked up at Buckskin. "He's not at all the kind of a man who excites me."

They turned the corner but she didn't relax her hold on his arm.

"We're heading for our horses, I guess," he said. "At least we put a dent in the Lombard hold on the county. If only that Attorney General can find Sheriff Lombard and arrest him. I don't have much hope for that, but it's something to pray for."

She looked up at him as they walked, holding his arm tightly against the side of her breast. "Did you really burn down the big barn over at the Black Kettle?"

"Now who said anything about that?"

"Jody. He was still so excited about it after he woke up this noon that he couldn't wait to tell me."

"I heard the barn had a bad case of spontaneous combustion from some green early hay they had cut and put inside."

Mitzi laughed and in a quick motion, reached up and kissed him on the cheek. "First rule of fighting the Lombards. Never tell them anything that is going on. Let them guess and wonder."

She frowned for a minute and took a long deep breath. It was almost a sigh. "Now all we have to do is figure out what we're going to do next."

"Easy," Buckskin said. "We sell those hundred head of steers before they get lost in the fighting. I'd say you can use four-thousand dollars about now. Cattle here still going for around forty dollars a head from what I heard."

"When?"

"Tomorrow. You have any friends in town where you could stay for a couple of hours?"

"Sure, why?"

"I'll hit a saloon or two and hire eight men for the drive tomorrow. We don't need them for the cattle, but we need a show of force in case the Black Kettle crowd gets any ideas about stampeding the herd again."

"Rifles?"

"Every man. If the men don't own a long gun, I'll have them borrow or rent one here before they come out."

They had reached their horses and she stopped and looked up at him.

"Three," she said, her voice low, her face serious.

He frowned a moment. "Three? Three what?"

"In the past two days, you've . . . you've killed three men. Doesn't it bother you? Those men had mothers who will mourn them, they might have had wives and children."

He took her shoulders with his hands and turned her to face him.

"I don't like the killing. It just seems to be part of my life when I get mixed up in this kind of fight. Usually I'm a detective. I track down killers, kidnappers, bank robbers, anyone someone else wants found.

"Yes, I killed two men at your ranch, and one today. It wasn't something I wanted or liked to do. But when a man fires a deadly weapon at me, he's telling me that I have a right to shoot back. If I shoot straighter than he does, then he dies instead of me.

"One of these times I'll be a little slow or a little bit wild and the other guy will be standing there looking down at my bleeding, dying body. It's something that every man who takes a gun in his hand has to think about.

"The secret is not to dwell on it. Yes, three men are dead, but they would have killed you and your brother and every hand on the place if they'd had the chance. That man today had three helpers with orders to kill me. I can't mourn for him or for the other two. I take life as it comes. I don't ask too much in return."

"Why did you stay? You didn't have to help us find the cattle, or come here today. You told me there was a wanted poster on you from here once. But it isn't around any more. Good. There's nothing to keep you here. Why get mixed up with us, as you put it?"

He pulled her gently to his chest and put his arms around her. He hugged her tenderly as if she were a delicate flower he didn't want to crush, then let her free. She hovered there a moment when his hands left her. She dropped her arms which had gone around him and then leaned away from him.

"I like you. Also, I don't enjoy seeing some big outfit walk all over a small ranch. I especially despise a sheriff who uses his office to trample the rights of other people and make his own fortune as he does it. Besides, I'm an easy mark for a pretty girl with a fine figure who lets me hug her and who kisses me on the cheek." He grinned.

"Now, let's ride to that friend of yours. I still need to hire eight trail drive cowboys."

Two hours later, Buckskin had hired the eight men. He selected them by their hands, not what

55

they said. He inspected their hands for rope burn scars, calluses, hurt fingers, split knuckles and even new rope burns. Those were the working cowhands.

He told each to report to the Box R at nine o'clock the next morning with a rifle, horse, two ropes and a six-gun. It would be a one day job.

"This a war or a cattle drive?" a man who looked like he could be a top cowhand asked Buckskin.

"Might be a little of both before we're done," Buckskin said.

The hand grinned. "I'll be there prompt," he said.

The ride back to the ranch in the dark went without incident. They talked a while. She told him about her early days and then the last ten years on the ranch. Her mother died of an outbreak of smallpox three years before. Then they remained silent listening to the night birds, and the occasional howl of a lonesome coyote in the distance.

At the ranch, she put her own horse away and hung the saddle in the barn.

"You can stay in the spare bedroom. Our foreman usually lives in the ranch house."

"That was when your father was alive. Wouldn't be proper now, and I wouldn't feel right. I'll bunk down with the hands. What time is breakfast?"

"Six o'clock as, usual. We won't take the chuck wagon along. We only have a ten mile drive and should get there before one o'clock or so."

"If we don't run into any problems."

"Meaning Black Kettle riders?"

"True. If we get the eight riders from town, we'll keep two of your hands here to guard the place. Can't see Fowler taking the barn burning without some kind of a response."

"He can't know who set the fire," she said.

"Yes, but he can guess."

They had walked to the house and now paused at the back door. The small overhang made a deep shadow. She pulled him into the darkness and kissed his lips gently. She sighed, then eased away.

"I've been wanting to do that all day," she said. "I hope you don't mind."

"Don't mind at all. I enjoy kissing pretty women, even if one of them is the boss." He stepped back. "See you for breakfast."

The next morning, Mitzi had a trail drive sized breakfast ready for the crew: country fried potatoes, eggs over easy, flapjacks, a platter of bacon and sausage, syrup, piles of toast and jam and all the coffee they could drink.

The new hands began riding in shortly after eight and Mitzi had coffee and cinnamon rolls for them. Buckskin inspected each man's outfit, his ropes, gear and his weapons. Seven men showed up. Buckskin had told them it was a one day job and they'd each earn five dollars for the work. If there was any shootouts, the pay would go to ten dollars. They'd be released when the cattle were safely in the shipping pens in town.

At 9:15 they left for the west range where they had kept the herd. Mitzi went along as Buckskin figured she would. One man riding guard on the herd reported no trouble. He went along with the crew and the seasoned cowhands quickly formed up the herd into a string three or four animals wide and about a hundred yards long. It would be a small herd to drive and they had plenty of help.

Buckskin put Jody in charge as the lead scout to move the cattle over the wagon road and toward town. They had to pass within half a mile of the Black Kettle spread. Buckskin rode a wide outrider post and watched for anyone from the other ranch who might be interested in their drive.

They came even with the Black Kettle and worked past it. Buckskin saw no sign of any unusual activity. He grinned when he saw six black, wooden beams that reached skyward from a mass of charcoal where the big barn had stood.

Mitzi kept near the front as a flanker to push any strays back into the line.

When they came to within half a mile of town, Mitzi and Buckskin rode ahead to talk to the railroad man. The agent in charge at the Boise rail yards was also a part-time cattle buyer for an outfit in Portland. He told them what pens to use and met them there when the steers arrived.

He inspected each animal and accepted them all. Mitzi explained the ten steers that had their brands blanked out.

"Heard something about that," the man said. "Hear you charged the sheriff with rustling."

"Indeed I did, and I want to see him stand trial. Not the first time he's ordered his men to rustle cattle off me and some of the other smaller outfits."

"Might be a tough call, getting Sheriff Lombard into a jail cell. But I wish you luck."

A short time later, Mitzi had a bank draft for the sale of the 104 steers. The price today was $41.50, and the draft showed a figure of $4,316.

"That's going to have to run the ranch for another year," Mitzi said. "I don't know what we would have done if you hadn't brought the cattle back from the Black Kettle."

"You ready for some food?" Buckskin asked.

"I don't know. After our last experience eating here, I don't think so."

"You going to the bank?"

"Yes. Where can I meet you?"

"I want to talk to Blackhawk again. Is Kurt the blacksmith still in town?"

"Oberholtzer? You bet. He's indestructible. Probably pounding away on some red hot iron right now."

"Meet you at Blackhawk's place. I'll use the back entrance. I don't want to run up against the sheriff until somebody puts him in jail."

Buckskin stepped down at the back entrance to the blacksmith's shop and saw the big man whaling away with his heavy hammer.

"Don't break it!" Buckskin shouted between blows.

The big man with sweat staining his forehead turned around, surprise on his flat, heavy face.

"Be good goddamned! Heard somebody was in town using your name. It's you in the body. I'll be good goddamned!"

Buckskin took the big paw and shook. The blacksmith dropped his hammer on the anvil and slapped Buckskin on the back.

"How long you been gone, ten years?"

"Twelve or more. This town has doubled in size."

"Growing every day. More settlers coming in every spring. Getting to be too damn big a town.

I'm about ready to move out where I can have some peace and quiet and a little more room. There's a store selling lumber and nails less than twenty yards up the street."

"You haven't changed much, Kurt. Except you're a lot uglier than you used to be. How can that sweet little wife of yours stand you?"

He grinned. "She reminds me of that every day. You married? No, I guess not. Hear you tangled with the sheriff already. Just like old times."

They talked for twenty minutes, then Buckskin said he had to go see Blackhawk.

Kurt nodded. "Damned fine man, even if he is an Injun. Best saddle maker in the territory."

They shook and Buckskin rode another block, then went up the alley and into the back door of the saddle and shoe repair store. He grinned when the scent of the leather swept over him like a Pacific Ocean breaker.

He heard talk from the front room and found Mitzi there chatting with Blackhawk. She held something and a scowl ruined her pretty face.

"I just don't believe it," Mitzi said. She looked up as Buckskin came in through the blanketed rear door.

"Glad you made it here safely," Blackhawk said. "I figured before you had some small troubles with the sheriff, but now every triggerman in the territory is going to be out to claim your scalp."

"Why?" Buckskin asked.

Blackhawk held up a poster. It was a foot wide and eighteen inches high. Bold black letters told the story:

"REWARD, $2,000 FOR BUCKSKIN LEE MOR-

GAN, DEAD OR ALIVE. Morgan last seen in Boise on June 24, 1876. Wanted for the assault, battery and attempted murder of a peace officer, in this city, July 4, 1864. Contact the sheriff's office to claim the reward."

Chapter Five

Buckskin Lee Morgan looked at the wanted poster and shook his head. "The same damn made up charges as before. Lombard or one of his men must have found the old one." He ripped the poster into a dozen pieces.

"Well, I guess I'll just have to deal with it. Has he posted them yet?"

"All over town," Mitzi said. "On half the buildings out there. How can he expect to get away with it?"

"He hopes he'll get lucky. Either the posters will drive me out of town and get me out of the sheriff's hair, or somebody will gun me down and eliminate the threat to him that way."

The poster went on to give a complete description of Buckskin and to say he had been seen with the Box R riders.

Mitzi put her hands on her hips and scowled.

"We just won't let anybody drive you out of town or hurt you. For starters, we better get right back to the ranch. I've been to the bank and the men are paid off. Nothing to keep us here."

"Soon as it gets dark, I'll tear down every one of those posters I can find," Blackhawk said. "I know, the word is out, the damage done. But at least I can get most of them out of circulation tonight."

"Probably twenty men in town right now who have one of those posters folded up in their hip pockets with my description burned into their skulls and their trigger fingers ready."

Buckskin pushed out his hand and Blackhawk shook it firmly.

"I know what it means to have everyone looking for you," the Indian said. "Keep to the back streets."

"I'm in the alley," Buckskin said to Mitzi. "Where's your horse?"

"Out front," Mitzi said. "I'll ride around and meet you at the near end of the alley, then we'll circle around town and head north."

It was a good plan, but before Buckskin got out of the alley behind the saddle shop on his bay, a man stepped from the shadows and planted his boots two feet apart, his right hand hovered over the butt of his six-gun.

"Morgan, seen you ride in here, figured you'd be coming out sooner or later."

The man looked about thirty, unshaven, eyes just a little bleary, and his hat askew on his head. He stood on the right side in front of the horse and he could see Morgan's gun hand. Buckskin didn't answer. He kept the horse moving forward

63

until he was thirty feet from the man.

Buckskin's right hand jolted upward. His palm hit the butt of the Colt .45 lifting it. The tied down holster moved less than an eighth-of-an-inch. The weapon came into his hand. His finger slid into the trigger opening and his thumb dragged back the hammer cocking the weapon, turning the cylinder to a live round.

All of this happened in the blur of a fraction of a second, then the end of the muzzle cleared leather and Buckskin lifted it in a classic point and shoot motion and his finger stroked the trigger. The entire movement from first move to draw to fired shot took less than half a second. The bounty hunter standing in the alley had time only to take a stab at his six-gun. He caught it and had it lifted an inch upward before the heavy lead slug from Buckskin's Colt smashed into his shoulder and slammed him backward like a tumbleweed.

The man screamed, his revolver slid from his hand and he sprawled in the alley dust and dirt. He turned over so he could see Buckskin who still sat on his bay and looked down at the defanged gunman.

"Next time I'll kill you," Buckskin spat and rode on down the alley. He saw another rider edge into the slot but recognized Mitzi. He came up to her, replacing the round in his Colt and easing the hammer down on the empty cylinder.

Her brown eyes showed worry and her hands gripped the reins tighter than needed. "I thought I heard a shot," she said.

"Just one. Nothing to worry about. You all right?"

She hesitated. "Yes, fine." She paused and looked behind her. "Two men sat watching my horse when I went out from the saddle shop. They must have seen the Box R brand. When I mounted, they did too, and followed me. They stayed about half a block back."

Buckskin nodded. "Figures, that damn wanted poster! All right, what I want you to do is to turn around and ride out of the alley, go the same way you were headed and move at a nice steady canter. They'll keep following you and I'll be right behind them."

"Be careful."

He saw the worry, the concern, in her eyes. She took a quick little breath and tried a grin that didn't quite come off. "Okay, okay, I'm going. I'm going to start carrying my gun."

"Move, please get out of here."

Mitzi turned her mount and rode out of the alley mouth and without pausing, turned to the right and kicked the little roan into a canter.

Buckskin pulled his mount in back of a pile of cardboard boxes and trash behind a store's rear door. He was close enough so he could hear the two mounts moving past the alley mouth at a faster pace now. When they passed, he eased his six-gun back into leather and pulled out from behind the boxes. He moved the bay quickly up to the end of the alley and checked down the dirt street.

There were a few houses, some small businesses, and two men on horses cantering along behind Mitzi and not looking back. He kicked his mount into a canter as well and followed the pair down the street two blocks.

There Mitzi turned north out of town and the two men began talking to each other.

Buckskin drew his iron and kicked the bay into a gallop. He came up on the pair quickly. One of them looked back and grabbed for his six-gun. Buckskin fired a round over his head and he lifted his hands and let the horse slow to a stop. The second man had lifted both his hands as soon as he saw Buckskin bearing down on them with his revolver drawn. Both stopped.

"Ease those hog legs out of leather and drop them on the ground. Do it now."

A bite to Buckskin's words bode no argument. Both men lifted their six-guns and let them fall to the ground.

"Now kick out of your boots. Right now! I got no time to waste or I'll have to use some hot lead."

Ahead he saw that Mitzi had stopped and now walked her horse slowly back toward them.

"Drop your boots on the ground, gents. Come on."

"We didn't mean no harm, honest," one of them said.

"Just wanted to see where the lady went. Mighty pretty." It was the other man.

"Just happened that she had a Box R brand on her horse, and you just happened to figure out that the guy on the wanted poster might be there."

"Hey, nothing like that."

Buckskin fired another shot into the air. "Now, men, take your reins and we'll move ahead at a canter. We'll be moving out of town aways."

"Where you taking us?"

"Have to wait and see."

Buckskin kept the two riders ahead of him. They met Mitzi and she joined Buckskin behind them. They rode out two miles, then stopped.

"Dismount, bounty hunters."

They both stepped down wincing as their stocking feet hit the hard ruts of the trail. Buckskin moved his horse ahead, picked up the reins of the two animals and without a word kicked his bay into motion and galloped away from the two screaming men.

Mitzi laughed when she caught up with him. "Should have seen the expression on their faces as you rode away with their horses. They were screaming until they got red in the face."

"Give them something to think about. They can walk back and get their boots and guns, or walk forward and hope to find their horses. The mounts are both from the livery stable. They'll go back there when they get hungry."

"Are we away from all of the bounty hunters?"

"Not a chance. Wave two-thousand dollars in a man's face and he's wild crazy to collect. Two-thousand is more than six years' wages for a cowboy. Man would be stupid not to give it a try."

"You expect some more visitors?"

"Lots more. We might find some on the trail up ahead. Could be some already at the ranch waiting for us. Hard telling what we'll run up against from now on."

"Sheriff Lombard sure knows how to fight mean. I just wonder what else he has waiting for us?"

"It won't matter if we can get him arrested on those charges. No doubt he'd be convicted of rustling. Even if he isn't sentenced to hang, he'd get twenty years. That would give us time to get the ranch straightened around and making money."

"You think I should hire a ranch manager?"

"Either that or get a strong foreman who can do the same thing. Running a ranch as big as yours isn't easy. Your brother seems to be no help at all."

When they rode close to the ranch, Buckskin motioned to the west and they followed the small feeder creek that meandered through the place. It was the same one Buckskin had used that first day he dropped by for a quick look at the old Spade Bit Ranch. They rode up behind the brush until they were at the closest point to the Box R Ranch buildings.

"All looks calm and peaceful," Mitzi said.

"Yeah, but where are the hands? I don't see a single ranch hand doing anything. Most of the horses are in the corral, so where are the men?"

"Oh boy. I didn't even think of that. What do we do now?"

"Not we, you. Ride back down a quarter-of-a-mile to the main trail and go on into the ranch yard just like usual. See what you can find. If there are bounty hunters there holding the men under guns, you start a fire in the kitchen range and make coffee. Use lots of paper so there'll be white smoke pouring out the chimney. I'll know what to do then."

"You sure?"

Buckskin nodded, touched her shoulder and motioned for her to ride. When she left, he stepped to the ground and took out the Spencer rifle. He checked the magazine, full. He looked in the chamber and left it partway open so he could slide a round into the breech. That way he had eight rounds without reloading. He might need them.

Ten minutes later, he watched Mitzi ride into the ranch yard, and call out but no one answered. She took her horse to the corral and left the saddle on the middle pole, then walked to the kitchen door of the ranch house.

It wasn't two or three minutes later that Buckskin saw smoke billowing straight up from the chimney over the kitchen. So, they had company. He had no way of knowing how many. It would have to be at least two men. They would work together. A cool $1,000 a man wasn't bad for a day's work.

As Buckskin watched, the first traces of dusk settled over the high country. It would be dark in another ten minutes. He could wait. He picketed his horse in a grassy spot and where she could reach the water, then stared at the ranch buildings trying to work out his plan of attack.

He couldn't come up with one. He knew there must be at least one bounty hunter in the house since Mitzi had made the fire so quickly. But were there others in the barn, the well house, maybe in the bunkhouse with rifles ready to take him dead instead of alive?

The ranch house was the most logical target. At least one bounty hunter was there. He'd pound on the kitchen door, then run around to the front and try to slip in when the bounty men were covering the kitchen entrance. Should work. Once inside the house he'd just have to play it as it came.

Darkness swept over him and he lifted from where he had been sitting at the fringe of the brush and walked toward the rear of the ranch house. There was no moon tonight. He could only see the vague shapes of the buildings. No lookout could spot him in the darkness.

It worked the way he had hoped. After pounding on the kitchen door, he rushed to the front of the ranch house and slipped inside. There were no lamps burning in the parlor or living room. He edged up to the door leading to the big kitchen with its ten foot plank table and surveyed the people there. Three of the crew sat at the cleared table. None of them had guns in holsters. One cowhand was missing.

Across the kitchen near the big stove, stood a man with a sawed off shotgun. Mitzi stood by the stove and moved the coffeepot back to the front lids over the firebox.

A man stormed in from the back door and growled. He carried a six-gun with the hammer cocked. "Now what the hell was that all about? Nobody out there. I looked all around."

"I do have one more hand you haven't captured," Mitzi said. "He isn't stupid. He knows something is wrong. You expect him to just walk in and give up?"

"Be smart if he did. What time you say this outlaw is coming back from town?"

"He said he wanted to play a little poker and do some drinking. He laughed when he saw the wanted poster. Said he'd probably have to kill two or three more bounty hunters before morning."

"Better not try it with me," the man with the shotgun said. "Me and Bertha here can make most men kneel right down and pray. Damn glad that poster said dead or alive. Dead is a lot easier to get into town. Dead never runs away or jump you."

Buckskin decided the shotgun man would have to go first, if it came to that. Even with a killing shot from Buckskin, the man could still get off a round from the shotgun with a spasming trigger finger as he died.

Too big a risk. He'd have to get them outside. How? He grinned. A fire would do it. He left the house as quietly as he had come in, found two old cardboard boxes and some straw and made a pile of them twenty feet from the barn. One lantern full of kerosine sloshed on the pile set it up. He scratched a match on his pants leg, tossed it into the coal oil and straw and ran over by the well house.

The barn was thirty yards from the ranch house. The well house stood in between. He ran past the well house and pounded on the kitchen door. "Fire!" he bellowed. He said it three times, then sprinted for the well house with his Colt in his hand.

The door opened and Buckskin figured it was the six-gun man who looked out. Then Mitzi showed in the lamplight.

"It's the barn. You've got to let my men go and try to put it out. It's just starting."

"Damnit all. This isn't working out right," the gunman said. "Hell, all right, you cowboys, get out there and save the lady's barn."

The three hands sped out the back door and

71

raced toward the flames. By now it was easy to see that the flames were in front of the barn, but the man at the door didn't realize that.

Once the crew had left the house, Buckskin ran to the end of the kitchen and eased up toward the door. It opened away from him here and by now Mitzi had walked out into the night. The six-gun wielder stepped out as well to watch the fire. Buckskin clubbed him on the top of the head with the butt of his Colt and the man fell like a head shot steer.

Buckskin grabbed the man's six-gun, pushed it in his own belt and dragged him away from the kitchen. He rushed back to the door and peered in. The shotgun man had just put down a cup of coffee.

"Ted," the man inside called. "Ted, damnit, why'd you let them three men out of here? Now all we got is the woman. Ted, damnit, where the hell are you?"

Buckskin heard hard boot steps come across the plank floor. A moment later the smaller man with the shotgun took half a step out of the door and Buckskin clubbed the hand that held the shotgun. The heavy weapon dropped to the ground.

Buckskin's hard fist slammed upward in an uppercut blow that lifted the shorter man off the porch floor and slammed him backwards into the kitchen. He hit on his back, his head thunking hard against the planks and was out like an empty coal oil lamp.

"You came after all," Mitzi said where she bent and pulled a six-gun from the unconscious bounty hunter's gunbelt. "I lied to them about you. I know it was wicked, but it seemed like the right idea."

"Finally made it. Tie his hands together in front of him, while I take care of his partner."

Buckskin moved back to the man beside the kitchen wall who was moaning and trying to sit up. He thudded his boot into the man's jaw just hard enough to discourage him. Then he flipped the bounty hunter over and took a tightly rolled rawhide thong from his pocket which he used to tie the man's hands behind his back. He used a second thong to bind his ankles together.

Back inside the kitchen, Buckskin finished tying the shotgunner's hands and then his feet. He picked him up like a sack of flour over his shoulder and carried him outside where he dumped him just beyond the first visitor.

Mitzi came out of the kitchen and rang the dinner triangle. The crew shouted from where they had the last of the bonfire put out near the barn.

"The men told me they hadn't eaten yet," Mitzi said. "Figure it's about time I get them some supper or I won't have a crew." She grinned. "How are our two friends? Should I fix something extra for them?"

"Don't bother," Buckskin said. "Come daylight and they wake up they're going to have a long naked hike back to town."

Mitzi giggled. "You wouldn't do that?"

"Don't bet on it. Maybe by morning I'll feel in a better mood and just shoot them a time or two and let them keep their clothes and boots for their walk to town. I might even give them a choice."

The missing crewman came back. He'd seen the two men ride in and fire at one hand and round them up and take them to the kitchen. The other hand was Jody and he said he wasn't about to get caught by a couple of rawhiders.

"Worse than rawhiders," Buckskin said later over his plate of supper. "Bounty hunters are the worst snakes that ever crawled on their bellies. Especially when they have a dead or alive wanted poster and it has my name on it."

"So what are you going to do with them come morning?" Jody asked.

Buckskin grinned at the young cowhand. The kid had a good head, used his brain. He might be a candidate for foreman of the ranch when Buckskin moved on.

"Do with them? Can't very well hang them, although I'd like to. If this was some big city like Chicago or New York, we could charge them with assault and kidnapping, since they held you here against your will. Most judges out here in the west don't hold much to them fancy Eastern kind of laws.

"Guess you'll have to wait to morning and see what kind of suitable punishment I can come up with."

By nine o'clock they had shut down the ranch. One man would keep watch from the well house and wake his replacement every two hours. Buckskin took the first watch from nine to midnight. The men went to the bunkhouse and he saw a lamp blown out in one of the upstairs bedrooms about ten minutes later.

Buckskin checked the two bounty hunters. They were awake and talking when he came up. Both bellowed in protest but Buckskin wouldn't even talk with them.

When he got back to the well house, he found Mitzi there shivering in the cool evening air.

"I had to see you," she said.

"I've seen you most of the day," he said chuckling.

"Thanks for saving my crew and me. That one with the shotgun is a killer, I can tell."

"He won't hurt anyone for a time."

"Something else." She moved over and stood directly in front of him so close they almost touched, but not quite. "I wanted to thank you another way."

She leaned up and kissed his lips and then eased away. "Mmmmmmmmmm." She watched him. "I think I liked that. Could I try it again?"

She kissed him again and this time her arms went around him. She touched him with her shoulders but not her breasts and hugged him gently. She kept her lips closed for the kiss and so did he. His arms were at his sides.

"Yes, I think I like that. I want to try it again when we have more time and when I don't have to get to bed. If I don't get some sleep, I'll be a grouch all day tomorrow."

She paused. "Buckskin Morgan, you are a strange man. I kiss you twice and you don't say a word. Did you like it, hate it, want to teach me the right way? What?"

Buckskin grinned and bent and kissed her lips again, just barely touching them. His gentleness was enough to set up a spark of electricity that caused her to snap her eyes open in amazement and pull back.

"Yes, pretty lady, I liked it. I liked it too much. Now get yourself out of here so I can be a proper lookout for your ranch."

Mitzi grinned, waved at him and ran back to the kitchen door only touching the ground every other step.

Chapter Six

Buckskin was up at six the next morning and checked the last lookout. He hadn't seen anyone or heard anything. After breakfast they prepared for a day-long survey of the outlying ranges.

"We like to get one man to ride the back pastures every week or so to check on conditions, see if any animals are down or sick," Jody said. He had been taking leadership among the crew members. Buckskin liked what he saw in the young man.

Buckskin looked at the two bounty hunters. Both had been yelling since he got up. He nudged one with his toe. "You got a complaint, shotgun man?"

"Damn right. Ain't legal tying us up this way. I'm gonna swear out a complaint against you."

"Go ahead," Buckskin said. "The minute you step into the sheriff's office somebody is going to match you up with a wanted poster."

Buckskin untied the ankles of the two men and told them to get to their feet. They managed after a few tries. Being tied up all night had left them stiff and sore and unable to walk for a minute or two.

Then he untied their hands and told them to walk out behind the barn.

"Why you taking us out there?" the taller man asked.

"I never shoot bounty hunters where a lady can see," Buckskin said and the shotgunner swore softly.

Two of the crew came to watch. Both had six-guns.

Once the little parade made it behind the barn, Buckskin ordered the two bounty hunters to sit down and pull off their boots and socks.

"I ain't walking ten miles back to town barefoot," the tall man said. Buckskin ignored him.

"Now gents, strip right down to your birthday suits. I want you both stark naked in two minutes."

"Not me," the shotgunner bawled.

Buckskin sent a .45 round digging into the ground between the man's bare feet. He jumped around wide eyed. A moment later he took off his vest and shirt, then his pants.

"Your drawers, too, back shooter," Buckskin ordered. Both men looked at the three six-guns aimed at them, shook their heads and pulled down their underwear.

"Now take a hike," Buckskin said. "Go any direction you want to, just be sure to miss the Black Kettle Ranch or they might just roast you for supper. Now move." Buckskin shot twice in the air and the men walked away south generally toward town.

"Don't think you can come back and get your clothes, Buckskin called. We'll have a man follow you the first four or five miles. Next time you go bounty hunting, you remember to follow the law and the rules. If you don't hurry and get out of range, I'm going to open up on your white backs with my Colt."

The two men looked back, then trotted down past the last corral and into the virgin sod of the Idaho Territory valley. It would be a long walk back to town.

Mitzi stepped out from the small door in the back of the barn. "Is it safe to come out now?" she asked, looking at the bare backs of the two retreating bounty hunters.

"Almost safe," Buckskin said.

Mitzi laughed. "I bet it's a day or two before they try to take over another ranch to find a wanted man."

"First they have to find some pants off some woman's wash line," Jody said. "Serves them right."

"Come by the kitchen before you ride. I've made some sandwiches for you to take along."

Buckskin sent a man to tail the two walkers, and the rest of them mounted up, collected their lunch from Mitzi at the kitchen and were ready to head east to check the far side of the ranch. Mitzi and the trail man would stay at the ranch.

"Don't expect you'll have any more bounty hunters like those two. One or two might stop by, but they probably won't be vicious like those two were. We'll be back before sunset."

Mitzi nodded.

Almost an hour later and four miles out near some breaks and a small feeder valley angling up into the foothills, they saw some buzzards working. Three spiralled down from their own lookout high over the valley. Buckskin headed the team that way. While they were still well off, they could see the big hawks and other carrion eaters hard at work near a lone ponderosa pine.

They spurred up to the spot and discovered six yearling steers down. Buckskin rode straight into the corpses, scattering the birds, driving them off with a pair of shots from his six-gun. He got off his mount and studied the animals.

Two of them showed bullet wounds to the head, and two of the animals were so torn up by the hooked beaks of the meat-eating birds that they couldn't figure out how they died.

Ten minutes later the men mounted and the other three looked at Buckskin.

"My guess is that rifles dropped them all," Buckskin said. "Could have been target practice by some deer hunters, but that isn't likely way out here so far from the timber. We could circle the place for hours and might not find any hoof-prints of the killers. Instead, let's just head for the Black Kettle range. How far from here is that, Jody?"

The young man said about five miles due west.

"Tit for tat?" Jody asked. He rode up front beside Buckskin as they angled toward the Black Kettle range.

"About the size of it. Lombard must be giving the orders. This is getting damn close to a range war. He's got a bigger army than we do. I'll ask

Mitzi to hire some more hands. We need them for protection."

They found the animals with the B-K brand on them a half hour later.

"Take down the first six critters we come to," Buckskin ordered. "Brood cow, steer, yearling, anything. Each of you do two animals and then we'll get out of here."

The men pulled rifles from their boots and shot down five steers and one brood cow. The rifles cracked in the still Idaho mountain air, then all went silent and the cowboys turned their mounts and galloped away from the scene.

A quarter-mile out they slowed to a walk, then lifted the pace to a canter and headed back to their own range.

"Hated doing that," Jody said. "I know, tit for tat, but seems a waste of good beef. Hope we can get this all settled down and we can get back to pure ranching. A lot of things we can do with the Box R. I mean, it could graze another thousand head with no problem about grass or water."

"I agree. Talk to Mitzi about it."

Jody looked at him. "Hell, I'm just a cowhand. What do I know?"

"A tad more than Mitzi. Remember she got pushed into this job. Her brother couldn't do it. Now that I'm thinking about Claude, what happened to him? Haven't seen him around."

"Two days ago he went into town. He does that from time to time. I don't know if he gambles or whores or what, but when he gets back home after a week or so, he's really washed out and dragging."

"That's what I mean. He's no help to Mitzi. She

needs someone to lean on and get advice from. I ain't gonna be here forever."

"How much longer?"

"Don't know. Depends on when we can nail Lombard. A week, maybe two. You don't have much time."

They hit Box R land a half hour later and continued their survey of their cattle and the distribution. They found one case of black leg and Jody took a kit off the back of his mount and treated the brood cow.

"Should have that salve every day for three days, but doubt if I'll get out here tomorrow. She looks like a good breeder. Maybe I should send somebody out to do her again."

"Good brood animal like her is worth near two-hundred dollars these days," Buckskin said. "That's a good idea to get her treated all three days."

They found one lame steer, but between the four of them they decided it wasn't anything that could be treated. The animal would cure itself or it would die on the range. It happened now and then. A real veterinarian probably would know what the problem was, but the nearest one was in town, and he was so old he never went out into the field anymore which made him less than useless to the ranchers.

By the time they finished the rounds and made it back to the ranch, it was a little after six. Mitzi had supper ready for them, a vegetable filled beef stew that they would be eating for two days. It was seasoned just right and Buckskin had three plates of it with the juices soaked up in slabs of homemade bread. He pushed back from the table belching and apologizing.

"Best damn meal I've had all day," he said. The crew laughed. "Really, Mitzi, that was delicious. Hope we have some more tomorrow."

"Don't worry, we'll have stew until it comes out our ears," Jody said and the crew laughed again.

"Now that you're in such a good mood, I can tell you we'll do guard duty again tonight. I'll take it from nine to twelve, then two hour shifts until six. You work out who takes what shift. Just tell me who to wake up at midnight."

In the bunkhouse after supper, Buckskin had four games of checkers with Jody. They split two each and by then it was time for guard duty.

"We'll use the well house for our lookout tonight," Buckskin said. "Not much moon out there, so it'll be most a listening situation. I don't expect any trouble, but we could have a bounty hunter or two or some of the Black Kettle gang could pay us a visit. We'll have to be ready. Keep your rifle loaded and beside your bunk."

Buckskin checked in with Mitzi. She had finished the dishes.

"You should have one of the crew do the dishes for you," Buckskin said. "Rotate them so they do dishes for a week, then get off for three weeks. Oh, I'm wondering about a few more crewmen. If we get hit by the Black Kettle riders, they can send ten men again."

Mitzi nodded. "Been thinking the same thing. Tomorrow maybe we can go to town and hire four more men. I hate to take you in there with those posters around."

"Don't worry about them. We'll get the men and be out of town before anyone knows we're there."

Five minutes later he rested his Spencer rifle over the ledge on the well house and looked around. It was one of those nights when the moon had been skinny and low in the eastern sky, then dark clouds blotted out what little bounced light the moon contributed, so it was so dark Buckskin couldn't see more than a dozen feet in front of him. He walked a circuit around the barn, out buildings and the ranch house.

On the third trip he thought he heard something near the barn. He drew his six-gun and moved that way. A black form against the barn moved where no form should be.

"Hold it," Buckskin barked. "Don't move an inch or I'll blow five holes in your worthless hide."

The form froze in place. He moved up slowly until he could see more clearly. At six-feet he saw the small figure and then made sure.

"Denise Lombard. What are you doing here?"

"Just looking around. Hoping I could figure out where your bedroom was. I got lucky."

She stepped up to him and kissed his lips. Hers were open and her tongue attacked him until he capitulated and opened his lips as well. Her tongue drove into him. He came away gasping for breath.

"Denise, this is crazy."

"Crazier the better." She flipped back both sides of the unbuttoned heavy blouse she wore and he could see her bare breasts in the dim light. She took his hands and put one on each of her breasts.

"Oh, my yes, now this is much, much better."

"How can I stand guard when you're trying to seduce me?"

Her hands found his crotch and rubbed at the bulge behind his fly. "Darling, I don't want to seduce you, I just want you to fuck me until morning. Can't we arrange that?"

"You're shameless."

"Not either, I just want to be fucked. Right here, right now."

"Right out in the open in front of everyone?"

"I don't see anybody. Oh, all right, let's go out behind the barn."

Buckskin felt his blood heating, the lump behind his fly became a telephone pole. His hands devoured her big breasts.

He bent and kissed her and she crushed his hands against her breasts trapping them. Her arms went around him and her crotch pounded against his, then did a hard rub in a circular motion.

Buckskin felt her heat penetrating him, it was like she was on fire and the fire licked at his groin, inflamed his hands, and set his brain rocking.

He pulled away from the kiss and caught her hand. "Not in back of the barn, in the barn, in the haymow. You ever been flipped in the hay before?"

He watched her in the darkness, then reached over and petted her breasts that swung free of her blouse.

"Sorry, silly question. Come on, in the small door and be quiet. We don't want half the crew out here."

She grinned at him and patted his crotch. "Tell them to get the fuck out and find their own girls."

It was darker in the barn, but they really didn't need any light. He found a blanket to throw down on the hay but she shook her head.

"I want to feel the hay on my back and my butt," she said and laughed softly. "I want to feel the whole damn thing from start to spurt. Now suck my titties."

Buckskin sucked her breasts and she slumped in the hay, taking him with her. She crashed into the four feet of hay, sank in then came up a little. He kept chewing on her breasts making her quiver. She pulled up her skirt and yelped at the touch of the sharp ends of the cut hay on her tender buttocks and thighs.

Her hands clawed at his crotch, pulling the buttons open, pushing down his pants.

"Do me quick Buckskin, or I might just curl up and die wanting you so bad. Hurry."

He spread her legs and lifted them, went between them and found the right spot. As she grinned at him in the half light, he drove into her.

Denise shrieked. He got his hand over her mouth hoping the men in the bunkhouse still playing poker hadn't heard. Buckskin wasted no time on her wants. He plowed ahead, came all the way out and stormed back into her slot bringing a grunt of satisfaction each time from her.

Then he lifted her knees and put her bent legs against his chest and pounded into her with hard thrusts that edged her higher in the hay each time.

She exploded in a climax before he felt his own

coming. She wailed softly and squirmed on the hay, driving upward with her hips, then panting and crying and wailing through a long series of spasms and shivers and more spasms that left her out of breath and gasping for more air in her lungs.

He kept punching into her during her climaxes and just before she stopped he found his own satisfaction and jolted against her soft form a dozen times before he panted and rolled away, so exhausted for the moment that he knew he couldn't move if somebody surprised them.

No one did. They both rested.

Five minutes later, she rolled over on top of his naked body and kissed his nose.

"My daddy is furious with you and Mitzi. He claims you've been the cause of all his problems at the ranch and in town. He says he's working up something special for you."

"He put up the wanted posters?"

"Yes. I told him he should have a picture of you on it, but he said he didn't have one. Tonight he decided the wanted poster didn't work, so he's cooking up something else."

"What is it? What is he going to try next? Is he going to hit the ranch here, or try to find me in town?"

"Oh, I can't tell you that. I have to be loyal to my father."

Buckskin snorted. "You can't even spell loyalty. What is it going to take for me to do to get you talking?"

"Three more times. I've never done four in one night in my life. Did twice once. I want four or maybe five times."

"That will take half the night."

"So, we have all night. I don't mind. Just so I get away from here before daylight. Then I can tell you what my papa is planning for you, Buckskin Lee Morgan."

"You're a tease."

"I also have two things you want. One is my luscious, gloriously sexy body. The second is papa's plans. Again, right now again in the hay, then the rest of them outside on the ground on that blanket under the stars. I love to look at the stars as I'm getting poked."

The second time in the hay went slower, then Buckskin figured he better do some looking out. He buttoned up his pants and made a circuit of the buildings, watching beside each one for five minutes before moving on. It was eleven-thirty when he got back to the barn.

"In half an hour, I go wake up the next lookout," Buckskin said.

"Plenty of time for you to poke me again this time under the stars."

Buckskin caught one breast and held it. "No. We'll go find a spot down by the creek where you can screech like a wildcat if you want to. Remember we'll have a man on guard. We find a spot for the blanket, then I come back and wake up the guard and get him going."

"Then you pretend to go in the bunkhouse but you get your big prick down here and diddle me again, right?"

"Unless you want to tell me now what your father has planned."

She patted his fly. "You rest up junior there and don't let him get too soft. I'll be waiting for you naked as a new born kitten, just mewing for you when you get back."

Next man on guard was Jody. He couldn't fool Jody slipping out of the bunkhouse.

Jody levered a round into his repeating rifle and lay in on the well house.

"You take it from twelve to two, then wake up the next man."

Jody nodded.

"I'm not sleepy yet. Got me a hunch. I'm going to go down by the creek and look around. Might sit down and keep watch there for a while. If anybody attacks the place, they should come out of that line of brush."

"Good idea. Just don't go to sleep down there. You'll miss breakfast."

"No chance."

Buckskin angled for the stream a hundred yards up the current from where the blanket lay. That might help if Jody came that way. He crossed the chattering creek and hurried down the far side to where Denise waited. She was naked, and spread eagled on the blanket staring up at the stars.

He slipped up without a sound and reached out and grabbed both her breasts. She didn't even jump.

"About time you got back," she said. "I damn near started number three without you."

Buckskin needed a little more encouragement this time but jolted his seed into her and they came apart resting.

He sat up and caught her shoulders.

"Now, you've got your record. What is your father working on?"

Denise giggled. "Hell, big cock Buckskin, I don't

know. He never tells me nothing. I don't have the damnedest idea what he might try next. He's mad as hell though, and had his lawyer man out to the ranch and they talked half the morning in the den about something. Pa wasn't too happy when the legal man left."

"You're not much help, Denise."

"Nope, but I'm one damn good fuck." She reached for her blouse. "Damn, I guess that means the good fucking times are over for tonight."

"You tricked me."

"You like being tricked. Hey, if I find out what he's up to, I'll send a note to you. A kid, about twelve will do anything for me. He'll bring the note. He's our foreman's son and I let him touch my titties."

"You're shameless."

"Yeah, but it's one hell of a lot of fun. Walk me to my horse. She's a quarter-of-a-mile down the creek."

Buckskin did, then checked in with Jody saying he didn't see or hear a thing and was heading for bed. He slid under the blanket and thought about Denise again. Insatiable. Besides that, it was going to be a short night.

Chapter Seven

Early the next morning, Jody and Buckskin rode into town. Buckskin stayed at Harry Blackhawk's saddle shop for two hours while Jody put out the word about hiring new hands in the three biggest saloons. Anyone who wanted a job was to meet at noon at the Broken Spur Saloon.

Jody met them and took them one at a time into the alley where Buckskin talked to them. Again he checked the men's hands and picked the ones who showed rope burns and hurt fingers and calluses. He wanted real cowboys who knew their craft.

He and Jody agreed on four new men, told them to meet them a half mile north of town at 1:30; then Jody and Buckskin slipped into a small cafe and had dinner.

They heard the news a few seconds after they sat down. Sheriff Lombard had turned himself in to the Idaho Territorial Attorney General to face the rustling charge. The trial date had been set for the next day. The other two prisoners on the same charge were still in the Ada county jail and all three would be tried together.

Buckskin grinned. "Looks like we're going to have to come into town tomorrow to serve as witnesses."

"You can't testify," Jody said. "You'll be arrested on that spurious wanted poster."

"Right, I won't testify, but you and another hand on the ride can. Shouldn't be hard to get a conviction."

"Trials here are on the simple side," Jody said. "No fancy lawyer talk or shenanigans."

"Good, the quicker the better. Oh, Blackhawk said he tore down over fifty of those wanted posters on me. He spots a new one now and then and rips it down. So far nobody has called him on it."

"Good, that's a big problem we don't want."

They finished eating and went out the back door into the alley where they had left their horses to keep Buckskin off the street. Two men stood looking at the animals with their backs to the cafe door.

Jody pulled his six-gun and covered the two.

"Interested in buying a pair of good horses?" Jody asked. The men turned and Buckskin recognized Deputy Sheriff Gage Lombard with his pair of hoglegs.

Gage ignored Jody's gun. "You're under arrest, Buckskin Morgan. I'll ask you to hand over your weapon."

Jody laughed. "You joking, you damn crooked lawman? This Colt says nobody's under arrest. I want you to move slowly and unbuckle your guns and let them hit dirt."

"No," Buckskin said. "Defang the other man and put him across the alley. Gage and I got something to settle here. Might as well be right now."

Gage grinned. "Heard you was dumb, Morgan. I couldn't hope you were this dumb. I'm ready anytime you are, Buckskin."

The other man had moved away from Gage, and when Jody motioned, he lifted the weapon out of his holster and tossed it to Jody who caught it.

"You really want it this way, Gage?"

"Absolutely. Then I collect two-thousand dollars and get rid of you at the same time."

"I have no passion for Mitzi Roland. I told you that before. I'm just working for her for a few weeks."

"Sure, that's what I figured you'd say. You're with her all the time. I've seen the way she looks at you. Go ahead, outlaw. Draw anytime you want to."

Years ago an old gunfighter pounded into Buckskin's skull the idea that if given a chance, he should be the first to start a draw. Even a tenth of a second head start gives the first man a big advantage. A man slower on the draw could often outshoot a fast draw if the slow man could start the action.

Buckskin didn't waste any time. He set his feet apart, looked at Gage twenty feet away and drew. The young deputy could use his weapon. His draw was fast, but Buckskin's starting advantage and experience brought his six-gun up first and his automatic aim centered on his adversary's right shoulder.

His trigger finger squeezed off the round. The big slug tore into Gage's right upper arm, smashing the smaller bone and blasting part of the white bone out the far side of the flesh.

Gage's arm pivoted backward from the force of the round and his own revolver blasted but too late. It swung downwards and the round drilled into the ground near his right boot. He staggered backward, spun half around and went down to his knees, his left hand holding his right arm.

Gage screamed. His eyes went wild, then he fainted and fell forward with his face in the dirt. The scream choked off.

"You killed him!" the man who had been with Gage screamed.

"Just a shot up arm," Buckskin said. "You best pick him up and carry him over to a doctor. He'll take some mending."

Buckskin and Jody stepped into their saddles; then Jody tossed the other man his six-gun.

"Don't bother trying to use it," he said. "I pulled out the cartridges."

They rode out of town down two more alleys, then along a half built up street to the north trail. They found their four new hands waiting for them and rode on toward the ranch.

Jody looked at Buckskin with a touch of awe.

"Wasn't that kind of risky, aiming for his arm or shoulder that way when you had an easier shot at his chest?"

"Risky, but I figured he was slow enough I could take some aiming time. Worked."

"If it hadn't?"

"Then I might be the one on his way to the doctor or the undertaker. Man's got to take a few chances now and then. I don't relish killing, especially when the other man is as young as Gage. He could straighten out yet, who knows. Leastwise he won't be shooting at anybody for another six months."

"You going to town with us tomorrow?" Jody asked.

"Like to. I'd need a false beard and some spectacles. We'll see. I'll at least be at Blackhawk's place so I can find out what happens. I hate disguises."

Back at the ranch, Mitzi came running out to meet them.

"Lombard gave himself up," Mitzi called. "We had a messenger bring notices to appear at the trial tomorrow so we can testify."

"So much for my good news. At least I brought you four new hands." He introduced them to Mitzi as the ranch owner and their boss. "For now you'll be taking orders from me or from Jody if I'm not around. Find a spot in the bunkhouse and get settled in. Put your horses and gear away. Tomorrow you'll get a guided tour of the layout by the other hands."

At supper that night they had to have two shifts.

"You need to hire a cook," Buckskin said. "You're working yourself to death. How about one of your old hands to help you do the cooking?"

Mitzi wasn't sure. "I could ask Charlie, he's older and I hear him groaning now and then when he gets off his horse. He might take to a kitchen job."

She watched Buckskin as they stood alone in the kitchen. "Are you coming to the trial tomorrow?"

"I won't be able to testify, but I suggest you take Jody and one of the other hands who went to get the herd back. That should be enough testimony. That and what we can get out of the two rustlers."

"But you'll be in town just in case?"

"I'll go to Blackhawk's place and have him check on the trial from time to time. Shouldn't take long knowing western judges."

"No fancy talk, no lawyer tricks," Mitzi said. "Justice, quick and sometimes without mercy."

The next day the small courtroom in the Ada county courthouse was packed with spectators as the district judge rapped his gavel for quiet.

The bailiff read the charges and the judge had the three men stand up and make their plea. They looked at the lawyer who had taken their case just the day before. He nodded and they pleaded not guilty.

The district attorney, Neal Varick, and the defense lawyer, Ed Johnson, approved the twelve men who had been brought into the courtroom by the county clerk for jury selection. The men were all local citizens and some of them had voted. No time was taken questioning the jury members.

Varick put Jody on the stand first and he quickly recounted the discovery of the rustling, and how five men from the Box R responded, tracked the animals four miles into the Black Kettle ranch range and found six men working a nighttime branding operation.

"What were the men doing with the cattle?" the DA asked.

"Blanking out the Box R brands and putting the B bar K brand on."

"That's the registered brand of the Black Kettle ranch owned by Isaiah Lombard?"

"Yes sir, that's right."

"When you discovered the branding fire and your cattle, what did you do?"

"We fired one shot at the men, told them they were surrounded and moved in. Four men escaped. Two men in the firelight had no chance and gave up."

"One of the men was wounded?" the DA asked.

"Yes, one was shot in the leg with a rifle round."

"Is that man in the courtroom today?"

"Yes he is. The man with the bandage on his right leg at the defendant's table."

"Let the record show that the witness identified Zane Franklin." The DA paused. "Who was the other man you captured in the act of rustling and rebranding the Box R steers?"

"He's the other man at the table with the moustache and brown hair. I never knew his name, but he was the second one."

"Let the record show that the second defendant, Mr. Richard Horton, has been identified by the witness."

The district attorney looked at his notes.

"Now, Jody, you said that you didn't actually see these two men rustle the Box R cattle, but that when they were captured, they talked to you about it. What did they say?"

"Horton, the one not shot, said they had orders from their boss, Isaiah Lombard, to go across the property line and bring back the herd of about a hundred head of market ready steers from the Box R range."

"Did Mr. Horton say he worked as a cowboy for Isaiah Lombard?"

"Yes sir, he did. Said he'd been with Lombard for two years."

"And Isaiah Lombard ordered Horton to go steal, to rustle the cattle from the Box R and rebrand them with the B bar K brand?"

"Yes sir, that's what he told me."

The defense lawyer couldn't shake the cowhand's testimony.

Later when Sheriff Lombard himself was called to the stand by the defense he gave a far different story.

"Now, Mr. Lombard, you own the B bar K ranch. Is that correct?"

"Yes sir. Built it up from nothing in ten years."

"Are you the full time operator of the ranch?"

"No sir. I leave most of that to my foreman who's also my ranch manager. He does the day to day decision making and runs the outfit."

"How much time do you spend at the ranch?"

"I have a full-time job as a county employee. Sometimes I get out to the ranch on weekends. I am supposed to get one day a week off my job."

"Were you at the ranch on the day that these cattle from the Box R wandered onto your range."

"I object, your honor," District Attorney Varick said. "Wandering is an inexact word and calls for an opinion by the witness."

The judge scowled. "I agree, Mr. Johnson. Rephrase your question."

"Were you at the ranch the day talked about by your two ex-ranch hands?"

"No sir. I was not."

"How can you be so sure?"

"We had a knifing that day. A drunk in a saloon took a knife to one of the girls. She almost died. Case took up my whole day and half of that night in question."

The district attorney couldn't shake the ranch owner's story. In his closing statement, DA Neal Varick pushed hard on the idea that Lombard was lying to save his skin. He owned and operated the ranch. Many times he was there for a week at a time and was often accused of spending more time at his ranch than in his sheriff's office.

When the jury came back two hours later, it was almost four in the afternoon and they were tired. The foreman of the 12-man jury read the unanimous verdicts.

The two cowhands were found guilty of rustling. Isaiah Lombard was found innocent on the charge.

The judge eyed the defendants. "Mr. Lombard you are found innocent on the charge and are free to go." He stared at the other two. "You men have been found guilty, and while you said you were just following orders or you would lose your job, following those same orders could make you lose your life. Instead, I'm sentencing each of you to twenty years at the nearest penitentiary. Sentence to include time already spent incarcerated. This court is adjourned."

Blackhawk went racing back to his saddle shop and told Buckskin what happened at the trial.

"Figures. Looks like Lombard's lawyer earned his money. So did the members of the jury earn the pay they got from Lombard. How hard would it be to talk to the members of the jury?"

"Not all that hard. Best to wait until after dark. I know all but one of them. He's new in town but I'll have his name before supper time."

Mitzi and her two hands came in the saddle shop. Buckskin thanked them for their work. "Mitzi. I've got to stay in town tonight and talk to some people. You three better get back toward the ranch so no one will figure I'm in here. Buy some leather thongs or something and get away from here."

Buckskin faded through the back curtain as a man came in the front door. The customer looked around, asked about a saddle, then went out.

Five minutes later, Mitzi told Buckskin to be careful and rode for her ranch with her two cowhands. Jody asked to stay with Buckskin, but he said Blackhawk would be the best help that night.

The first man Buckskin talked to that evening was the Baptist preacher. He had been called to be on the jury by the county clerk and deemed it his civic responsibility.

"Render unto Caesar those things that are Caesar's," the preacher explained to Buckskin.

"Did anyone approach you before the trial? Did anyone offer you money to vote one way or the other?" Buckskin asked.

"No sir. I wouldn't have held with any behavior like that." He paused. "I see what you mean. Knowing I'm a man of God, they wouldn't have bothered to talk to me. Yes. I see what you mean."

The next man on the juror list was Lanny Tabler. When they slipped into his house without knocking, Lanny had almost finished packing a carpetbag. He jumped when Blackhawk opened his bedroom door and walked in unannounced.

"Damn Injun!" he brayed.

Buckskin moved around Blackhawk and asked him the same question he asked the preacher.

"Hell no, nobody offered me money. That's illegal. No time to do that. We was only contacted two hours before the trial started. Well, some of us were talked to last night."

"How much did he offer you, Mr. Tabler?" Buckskin asked.

"I don't have to listen to this. You get out of my house, right now."

"Why are you packing?"

"My brother took sick in Cheyenne. I got to get over there and help run his hardware store."

"Looks like your purse is bulging, Mr. Tabler. I wonder how much cash money you took out of the bank for your trip?"

He picked a wallet off the dresser and opened it. A sheaf of cash fell on the bed. Tabler grabbed for it but Blackhawk's big knife hovered in front of the juror's throat and he eased back.

A moment later Buckskin finished the count "Five hundred and eighteen dollars. The price for a jury member has gone up. You're going for a trip all right, Tabler, but not to Cheyenne. You're going to talk to the District Attorney."

That night Buckskin and Blackhawk found three more jurors who had wads of money on them or in their homes and each had urgent travel plans. By midnight, Buckskin had the four men stashed away in a locked room at the District Attorney's office. The DA said he would have them guarded there that night, and put in jail first thing in the morning along with new charges against Sheriff Lombard of jury tampering and bribery on four counts.

Buckskin and Blackhawk walked down the deserted main street toward the Indian's office and living quarters overhead. Only three saloons were still open. Blackhawk slowed when they past the splash of light from lanterns in the last saloon. He stepped into the blackness of the close by alley and pulled Buckskin in with him.

"Company," he whispered. They waited a minute, then another, and Blackhawk edged out and took a look around the wall. No one was there, the boardwalk was empty.

They continued on to his shop, unlocked it and went inside.

Blackhawk had just lit the coal oil lantern when the street door rammed open and Slash Wade burst into the room with a six-gun in his hand covering the two men.

"Well, well, well. Our redskin ridiculous excuse for a man has teamed up with Buckskin, a poor excuse for a white man. I been waiting a long time to settle things with you, Morgan. Looks like the time has finally arrived." He motioned with his heavy six-gun.

"Gents, drop your hardware, your guns. Buckskin, don't forget the big one and your hide-out and you, Injun, lower that stabber to the floor nice and easy. Do it now before I lose my temper and start shooting."

Chapter Eight

The man with the gun leveled at Buckskin grinned. "Just in case you don't know who I am you big turd, I'm Slash Wade. I heard what you did to Gage, bushwhacked him. Shot him from hiding like the cur that you are. Now we're gonna even things up a little."

"No bushwhack," Blackhawk said. "Gage had a partner and I was there. It was a fair fight. Gage was just a little bit slower."

Wade grinned. "Damn fine. Good news. Now I'll know that I'm faster than Morgan, cause I'm gonna give him a chance. Usually I don't play these games. Gage and me used to shoot balloons, see who could bust the balloon first. I almost always won. So I'm faster than Gage. Faster than anybody in the whole damn territory."

"That must make you the sheriff's main trigger man, right?" Buckskin asked.

Slash laughed. "I've been known to do a job now and then for the sheriff. Usually it don't take no gunplay, just gentle persuasion."

"So you've got a reputation in town," Buckskin said. "You going to gun me and then claim you're faster than me? No witnesses. Shouldn't this be done in the middle of main street with half the town watching?"

"Didn't work out that way. Hell I've got a good rep now. All I want to do is get this job done."

"A job given you by Sheriff Isaiah Lombard?" Blackhawk asked.

"Maybe, maybe not. No damn concern of yours, Injun." Slash said it with anger but never took his angry stare from Buckskin.

"You really want to try me, Slash? If you do, let's go over to a saloon, have some witnesses and do it right."

The big man holding the gun frowned evidently thinking about it. At last he shook his head. "No, it's some trick you have. I won't give up my advantage. You, Indian, lay flat on the floor over there by the counter. Morgan, move up to the front door. I'll be back here. That's fifteen feet. Nobody can miss at fifteen feet. Man who draws fastest wins. The other one gets buried. Move it, men, right now or I don't give either one of you a chance."

Both of them stepped to their assigned positions. Buckskin stood with his feet apart, his right hand twitching near his leather holster, the Colt free and loose in its home.

Slash moved back three steps and jammed his own six-gun into the holster.

"Anytime you're ready, there—"

Buckskin drew his Colt and fired. The sound of the two gunshots came almost together. Buckskin's hammer fell a fraction of a second sooner than Slash's. As he had drawn his weapon, he took a step forward pushing his left foot to the right in line with his right foot and turning his left shoulder toward the other gunman. It made a sideways target for Slash to try to hit much like a half crouched sideways dueling position.

Buckskin felt more than heard the roar of the two six-guns in the small room. The sound deafened him. He sensed the splash of air as Slash's bullet whispered past his shoulder and directly where his heart would have been if he hadn't turned and stepped forward.

He heard a high scream through the roaring in his ears. Slash took Buckskin's round in his chest, staggered back two steps, lost his balance, tumbled to the rear, smashed into the counter and bounced off it to the plank floor.

He was dead by the time Buckskin knelt beside him. He rubbed one hand over his face.

"Damn. He was a fool. There was no other way."

Blackhawk nodded. "He was fast sure enough. Near as fast as you were. I've never seen that forward step move before. Did you hear his bullet?"

"Heard it? Almost ate it. Missed my shoulder by not more than an inch. If I hadn't moved, we'd both be dead by now."

"We'll take him out the back. I got a horse out there. I'll pack him out of here and a mile away from town."

"Self-defense. Shouldn't we go to the sheriff, or at least to the Attorney General?"

"Not this time. You have troubles enough."

"I better get out to the ranch, get an alibi." Buckskin nodded, seconding his own motion. "Yeah, I better ride."

"I'll come out tomorrow and let you know what the Attorney General is doing about that jury bribery charge. We better git."

They both rode.

Buckskin got to the ranch two hours later and rattled Mitzi's bedroom window. She came quickly.

"Something wrong?" she asked. She pushed up the double hung window and stood there in a thin nightgown. The front had been cut low. She bent to sit on the window ledge and even in the half light of the moon he could see her bare breasts when the neckline billowed out for a moment. She didn't seem to mind.

He told her quickly about Slash Wade's challenge and what happened.

"It gives me the shivers just thinking about it." She reached out and touched his face, brushing her hand along his jaw and to his blondish brown hair in back. "Do you want to come in for a while and talk about it?"

Buckskin grinned. "Don't think that would be a good idea with what you're wearing."

"If it bothers you I can take my nightgown off." Her brown eyes sparkled.

Buckskin shook his head. "Afraid not. Not that you don't look delicious. It's just not right. I better get some sleep. We'll find out about the jury bribery charges tomorrow."

He reached up and pulled down the window. She reluctantly moved again giving him a view of her firm, heavy breasts down the top of her nightgown. It took Buckskin a few minutes to get to sleep that night.

A little after eleven o'clock the next morning, a rider came pounding into the Box R Ranch. He knocked on the rear kitchen door and gave a letter to Mitzi. She told him to wait and she'd get him some lemonade.

She read the letter and ran out to the corral where two men were working at gentling a wild horse they had roped up near the hills. Buckskin met her and she waved the letter.

"From Blackhawk. There's a notice up that the Box R is going to auction on a sheriff's sale to satisfy a judgment against the property for unpaid taxes. It can't be. I've never received a tax bill of any kind. Pa warned me to pay our taxes right on the date due."

"We better get back to town," Buckskin said. "I'll saddle your horse. We'll go see Blackhawk. There could be some trouble."

They rode into Boise just after noon after pushing their mounts. Buckskin found one of the notices tacked to a building and tore it down and gave it to Mitzi. She read it and passed it back to Buckskin.

"Auction on the courthouse steps at three this afternoon. Gives us some time. I'll check with Blackhawk. You go to the County Clerk and tell him you never received any kind of a statement. You brought your bank drafts with you?"

She nodded. "You be careful, Lee Morgan. Those wanted posters are still in a lot of pockets around town and the sheriff hasn't recalled them."

107

Buckskin went down another street, then up the alley in back of the saddle shop. Blackhawk had a shotgun trained on the back curtain when Buckskin walked in. He nodded and put down the weapon.

"Things been happening. Had a visit from the Attorney General. He's working on charges against the sheriff but says it'll take him until tomorrow. He needs a judge to sign some orders and the man is out of town."

"So he can't stop the sheriff's sale?"

"Not with what evidence he has now. I talked with the county tax collector. He was nervous as an old setting hen. He damn well took cash from Lombard to rig this. I don't know how he set it all up for the sheriff, but he near wet his pants while I was asking questions."

"The tax bill is a hundred and twenty-eight dollars," Buckskin said looking at the notice. "Seems a lot of taxes for the county." He stared at the poster again. "I've seen these before. The sheriff makes the starting bid at the amount owed on the place. In some cases the county gets any money over that amount, but in most states and territories the legal owner gets the overage and the deed goes over to the new owner who won the bid."

"So somebody could buy the whole Box R spread for a hundred and twenty-eight dollars?" Blackhawk asked.

"That's the way most of the laws are written. Encourages people to pay their taxes."

"Can she get the auction stopped by paying up now?" Blackhawk asked.

"Seems reasonable, but most times that doesn't

work. Too late by that time and the procedure has to be carried out."

Blackhawk shook his head. "By now I must be half white, but I still can't figure out how one person can own the land. The land is Mother Earth. How can someone own what's been here for hundreds, even thousands of years? The land should belong to everyone."

"I understand what you're saying, but the white world just doesn't work that way. Oh, any reaction yet about Slash Wade?"

The Coeur d'Alene Indian kept working on a saddle and shook his head. "Don't reckon anyone has found him yet. No worry about him. No big loss to the town. The sheriff will be mad, but most nobody else."

"Seen any more posters or bounty hunters around?" Buckskin asked.

"Found two more posters early this morning. Used them to start the fire for my coffee."

Buckskin walked back and forth in the small shop. At last Blackhawk grinned at him. "You better go take a walk outside before you wear my floorboards into pieces."

"I should have gone with Mitzi to see the tax collector and the county clerk. But, I guess that wouldn't have been so smart. I don't know if that damn poster has any official standing or not. They'd usually need to have a warrant or some kind of paper to issue a local wanted that way."

Blackhawk only grinned at him.

"Okay, okay, I'll go see who I can find down Main Street," Buckskin said."

"Keep your hat low over your eyes, white man,

and watch your scalp. Probably nobody will recognize you."

Buckskin left the saddle shop and walked half a block down the main artery of Boise. He found more than a dozen new stores that weren't there when he left twelve years ago. One sold nothing but men's clothing. A haberdasher way out here in the wilds of Idaho, imagine that.

He passed a saloon and almost went inside, but resisted the temptation for a beer. The courthouse came next. He crossed to the other side of the street to stay away from it and looked in the window of a land office. He didn't know if it was a government land office to record land sales or if it was a local man trying to trade on the name and sell land and houses on his own.

He had just turned around when a man standing near him called out his name.

"Morgan. Buckskin Lee Morgan. Damn that's got to be you and I'm two-thousand dollars richer."

He stood twenty-five feet away and held his hand near a well used six-gun on his hip.

"Richer or dead," Buckskin called.

The man was nearly as tall as Buckskin's six feet, lean, and looked hard bodied. He had a well used low crowned ranch style cowboy hat on and wore jean pants and jacket.

"Where I come from, partner, men who are men back up their mouths with action."

"How much action can you stand?"

"How much can you give?"

Buckskin sighed. Half a dozen men and three women had gathered to watch the little drama.

"Before you do anything stupid, let me give you a little demonstration. Find yourself a hand-size rock or a dirt clod. You hold it out at arms length and shoulder high and drop it. As soon as it leaves your hand, I'll draw and fire and blast that clod into a thousand pieces before it hits the ground."

The thin man with the dark hat hooted. "Hell, no human on earth can do that. Nobody can draw and shoot that fast, let alone hit a small target like that."

"Find the clod or move along," Buckskin said his voice rasping with anger and impatience.

A little boy ran out from the edge of the street and gave the cowboy a clod about fist sized. The man looked at it, then at Buckskin. "We'll move over here by the alley so your bullet won't tear up nobody," the challenger said.

They both moved and the other man shook his head. "Gunsharp, if you can bust up this clod on a dead draw like that, I'll fold my tent and slip away and you won't hear another damn word out of me."

"Hold it out", Buckskin said. He set his feet and his right hand quivered over his Colt. "Drop it whenever you want to."

Almost at once the cowboy let go of the clod. It fell straight for the ground. Twenty feet away, Buckskin drew and fired. His bullet blasted the clod apart a foot from the ground. A dozen men and women cheered. The cowboy with the dark hat and loud mouth stared at the puff of dust a minute, shook his head and turned and walked away.

"How you do that, Mister?" a towheaded boy of ten or twelve asked.

"Practice, son, lots and lots of practice. But I

hope that you never need to do that much practice with a six-gun."

He walked on. No one else bothered him. He toured one side of the street, then came back and saw Mitzi hurrying out of the courthouse.

He caught up with her.

"So?"

"He said I was too late to make the payment. Nothing the clerk could do to stop the sale. He said my only hope was to outbid everyone else and buy back my own spread."

"So, it depends on who bids against you." Buckskin began to grin. "Might not be a lot of folks on hand at three this afternoon. Let's have a bite of lunch as they say in San Francisco, and think about this."

They ate at a cafe where Buckskin had his back to the wall and plenty of open space around him. He faced the door and checked out everyone who came in. No trouble.

After the meal they went back to the saddle shop.

"Heard you dazzled the guys in the street with some fancy shooting," Blackhawk said.

Buckskin shrugged. "Better than killing somebody. Sometimes I miss and it doesn't work out so well."

Mitzi raised an eyebrow and Blackhawk told her about it.

At 2:45 that afternoon, Buckskin, Mitzi and Blackhawk came to the courthouse by different routes. Only three people stood there waiting for the auction. Mitzi stared at each of them and then went to one and began talking about the situation. One man shrugged. The next man she talked to was angry at the county clerk for making such a foolish mistake.

The three friends did not seem to notice each other. Mitzi would bid. Buckskin and Blackhawk would attempt to discourage any one else from bidding.

By three o'clock, the sheriff walked out of the courthouse with a folder and held it up.

"Ladies and gents, we're here today to offer at a sheriff's foreclosure auction the property known as the Box R ranch, for a short time yet owned by Claude and Mitzi Roland. The minimum bid is the amount of the tax bill, one hundred and twenty eight dollars. Do I hear an opening bid?"

"Just a minute!" Mitzi shouted. She went to the top step. "I'm Mitzi Roland and I own the Box R. I want everyone here to know that there is some kind of illegal, skulduggery going on here. The county tax collector never sent me a statement that I owed taxes. The county clerk said he had no idea my ranch was in a late payment stage. He said usually the county puts a late charge on the bill and resubmits it.

"This wasn't done either. There is a conspiracy here to steal my ranch from me. It's worth far more than the one hundred and twenty eight dollars, and the sheriff and the tax collector know that.

"This is an illegal auction, and the sheriff is about to be arrested again for illegal activities. He's rushing this sale through before he lands in jail again."

"That's enough, Miss Roland," Sheriff Lombard shouted. "Don't say another word, or I'll have a deputy remove you from these premises. Now, who will make an opening bid for one hundred and twenty eight dollars?"

"I'll bid that much," a voice came from the side. Buckskin moved that way. By then there were thirty people around the steps.

"I have a bid of one hundred and twenty-eight dollars. Do I hear a hundred and fifty?"

"I bid a hundred and twenty-nine dollars," Mitzi shouted. The sheriff ignored her.

"Another bid was made, a voice shouted from the back. You've got to recognize it."

"I said I bid a hundred and twenty nine dollars," Mitzi called out again.

The sheriff scowled. "All right a bid of a dollar more. Do I hear another bid?"

"A hundred and fifty," a young man shouted from the side. By then Buckskin saw who it was and hurried up beside him. Gage Lombard stood there with his right arm in a white sling and a heavy cast on it. He was the one bidding. Buckskin eased up on his good side and pinned his left arm to his leg, then pushed a hide-out derringer against his side.

"A hundred and fifty one dollars," Mitzi bid.

The sheriff recognized it with a slight smile and a nod. He looked over at his son. "Any more bids?"

Gage Lombard started to say something. Buckskin rammed the small automatic against his side harder.

"You really tired of living, kid? Is that your trouble? I can shoot you and be gone in a second and no one will figure out who slaughtered you."

Gage didn't bid.

"I have a hundred and fifty one dollars for the Box R ranch and the approximately six hundred head of cattle. Do I have another bid?"

"Hell no," somebody shouted from the back.

"Another bid for this valuable property, please."

"You bid on it, sheriff, before you wind up in jail again," a third heckler called.

"I'm the winner," Mitzi shouted.

"Say it's sold, Sheriff, or we'll say it for you." The voice was that of Blackhawk who ducked down when the sheriff looked his way.

"All right. Going once. Going twice. Sold for one hundred and fifty one dollars. See the county clerk with your money and claim your ranch."

Sheriff Lombard walked down the steps and angled toward his son who stood where he had been, only now Buckskin was no longer beside him, wasn't even in sight.

"What the hell?" he shouted. "What the hell happened to you?"

Only a few people were still around as the sheriff and his wounded son walked off toward the county offices.

One of them was Buckskin Morgan who chortled and grinned as he saw the sheriff screeching at his offspring.

A half hour later, they met back at the saddle shop. Mitzi had paid the $152 and got a receipt and a legal transfer of property ownership from her and her brother. Now the ranch was solely in her name.

None of them had heard anything about Slash Wade.

"Maybe nobody has found him yet," Buckskin said.

Mitzi nodded grimly. "Let's not ask for trouble. We've got some ranch work piled up out north aways that we better tend to." She went over and gave the big Indian a hug. He shied away from her, then let her hug him and stepped back, his face red, his hands worried about what to do.

"Thanks, Blackhawk. I owe you two guys so much. I guess I should put Blackhawk on the payroll, too."

The Indian feigned surprise. "Too? You mean this lout is getting paid to help a pretty girl like you? He had me fooled."

They all laughed and Mitzi and Buckskin went out the back door and found their horses where they had left them.

"In two hours we'll be back at the ranch, which is all mine now, by the way. We'll lay out the jobs that need to be done and you can assign the men. Wow, with eight hands it's a real luxury."

They rode along in silence for a while. She moved up close and touched his shoulder.

"Buckskin Lee Morgan I thank you again for your help. Without you there, Gage could have bid the place up out of sight and cost me thousands of dollars."

"Pretty lady. All the thanks I need is another one of those great smiles of yours and to know that you're happy on the old Spade Bit Ranch. Now let's get on home."

Chapter Nine

Morning came bright and clear at the Box R Ranch. The former cowhand helped Mitzi with breakfast for the crew, suffered some razzing from the three older hands, and took over to do the clean up after the meal was finished.

Mitzi, Jody and Buckskin conferred and got some work projects lined up for the crew. Buckskin and Jody parceled them out, then one went with each of the two crews to get the work done.

They had to drive some of the beef and cows and calves off the low ranges into the upper valleys where there would be green grass for a longer period of time. The job took most of the day, and when they got back they had word that Jody had treated that sick brood cow with salve on her black leg, and also made a new count on cows and calves.

After supper that night, Charlie took over the

clean up and dishes and Mitzi told Buckskin she wanted to see him about eight o'clock in the office. She had started using the term about her father's old den where he had all of the ranch records and account books and history of the place.

Buckskin took a walk around the ranch yard to get his legs limbered up after the long ride, then made it to the boss's office at precisely the right time.

She looked up from her account books and smiled when she saw him. "I do like a man who is prompt."

She showed him her plan to work the bulk of her herd higher and higher on the range until by fall her animals would be on the farthest north pastures and still finding green grass.

"Just when do I start bringing them back down?" she asked. "I remember that Daddy always used to do this automatically. He must have had some kind of schedule but I never saw anything about it. He had a set time for cutting the wild hay that grows along the stream where it overflows in the spring, too. We can cut it with a sickle bar mower. I saw one in town a week or so ago. They're brand new and work so much faster than four to six men can with scythes. I don't have any idea what they cost."

"You'll cut the hay and put it in the barn to feed this winter if the cattle get snowbound and can't dig down to the dried grass on the pastures?"

"What Daddy had to do twice, that I can remember. He said he saved half of his herd that way that otherwise would have starved to death."

"Lots of work hauling hay out into the pastures."

"We've got sled runners we put on two of our hay wagons. They have wide bodies built out to carry the light hay in big batches."

"Should work," Buckskin said. "When do you usually get your first snow here?"

"Any that sticks on the ground usually comes toward the end of November."

"So you want to have most of your cattle down before December. We'll work out a schedule of driving them down, just the reverse you use to get them up the slopes."

"Let's do that right now while you're still here."

They worked out both schedules. When they finished it was nearly ten o'clock.

"Well, that should do it for now. Oh, I want to show you something. It's a picture of my father. I want you to know a little about him. He built this ranch from nothing."

"Where's the picture?"

"Oh, I had it here but I moved it. Come along and I'll show you."

She led him down a short hall and into a room, her bedroom. She saw him hesitate at the door. "The photo was taken by one of those traveling photographers. It's quite good."

He went into the room and looked at the picture she handed him. When he took the picture she moved up close and put her arms around his back and reached up and kissed his lips. It was short and she came away.

"Buckskin, I've thought so much about our last kisses. Would it be too much of a struggle for you to try a few again?"

Buckskin smiled down at her, his chest pressed hard by her full breasts, her arms still tight around him.

"I don't think it would be a struggle. First, let me put down the picture."

He put it on the dresser and she held her arms around him and lifted her face. He kissed her hard on the mouth, crushing her breasts against his chest, bringing a soft moan from her. He didn't hold it long and watched her when he left her lips.

"Oh, my goodness," she said. "That was fine." She looked up at him. "Once more?"

She stretched up this time and kissed his lips hard and then softly and nibbled at them. Then she kissed him with her mouth open and her tongue jolting into his mouth and stabbing around. All at once her knees buckled and Buckskin was caught off guard. Both of them sat down hard on the bed and he was glad the bed boards didn't fall out of the frame.

She held the kiss and found his hand with hers. When she moved away, she lifted his hand to her breast.

"Like before, pet me a little. I want you so much it makes me jittery."

He caressed her breasts through the fabric, then unbuttoned the blouse and went inside. She wore no chemise. Her breasts felt hot to his hand, her nipples throbbing.

"Oh, dear. Oh, gracious. When you pet me that way it just makes me want to—"

Before she could finish, her body jolted and shook and vibrated as a thousand small sparks of electricity drilled through her flesh and bones, strumming her nerve endings and bringing a moan of total joy from her.

She looked at him a moment wide-eyed, then felt the darting needles of desire. His hands petting her brought another climax and then another and a fourth. She trembled and shook and when the last one faded away, her smile was so beautiful he had to kiss her. It was his almost touching lips kiss and she brightened her smile even more.

"Buckskin, I want to take all my clothes off, and take yours off, and I want you to stay here all night and teach me how to make love."

Buckskin let go of her and stood. "You're a virgin, aren't you, Mitzi?"

She nodded. "But now I want to make love with you. I want you to show me what to do and how to do it. I want to learn everything there is to know about sex and men and making a man happy."

Buckskin stepped back. "Those are things you'll learn with your husband. It's best for the two of you to learn together. That won't be me. I'm just here for a short time."

"I don't care, I want you right now. Can't you understand?"

"Yes, sweet Mitzi. I understand better than you know. That's why I'm walking out the door before this goes too far. You had a small taste of sex. Now just put it on hold and savor what you felt, and relive it and enjoy. There's no rush, no hurry. Just take your time."

He walked to the bedroom door. "I better get out to the bunkhouse. We have a long day of riding and cattle working tomorrow. You sleep well and have happy dreams."

She frowned at him as he went out of the room and closed the door.

It was just after breakfast the next morning that a young boy no more than sixteen rode into the ranch. His mount was lathered and blowing when he pulled her to a halt. He asked to talk to Buckskin Morgan.

Buckskin gave him a big drink of water.

"Now, son, what's this all about?"

"Message from Blackhawk. He's in jail. He said to tell you that he's been charged with molesting some young girl he swears he's never even seen. He asks if you could come in right away and give him some help, or he'll be tried and hung before sundown."

Jody was already on the range with four hands. Buckskin was getting ready to go out. He asked the boy if he'd had any breakfast. A shake of the head came and Buckskin caught his arm and led him up to the kitchen.

Inside he called to Charlie.

"A big breakfast for this new hand. Where's Mitzi?"

"Went to her room a few minutes ago," Charlie said. He looked at the young man. "You like eggs and country fried spuds?"

The youth nodded.

Buckskin angled across the kitchen to the hall door and hurried down to Mitzi's room. He knocked.

"Come in."

He told her the news and she began to pull off the work jeans she had just put on. Buckskin headed for the door.

"I'll get the horses saddled. Be ready to ride in five minutes."

Two and a half hours later, Buckskin and Mitzi rode into Boise and trailed alongside the county courthouse. They tied up their horses on the back side of the big frame building.

They had agreed that Mitzi would go in to the sheriff's office and get the particulars on the charges, then come back and they'd plan what to do.

Inside, Mitzi talked to a deputy who showed her the complaint signed by Arthur Denley. It charged that Blackhawk had molested his daughter, Opal Denley, 14. He had accosted her three times in the dark near their home, fondled her and made improper remarks to her about sexual matters. He let her go only when she screamed. The dates were given, one, two and three weeks ago on Saturday nights.

They wouldn't let Mitzi see Blackhawk who was being held in jail without bail until his arraignment the next day. Mitzi thought she knew the girl. Had seen her in school. She was only five years younger than Mitzi.

Back at the tie rack, Mitzi briefed Buckskin on the situation as they rode to the far side of town and stopped at a small house that was in need of paint and general repairs.

"This is where the Denley's live. The girl's mother died two or three years ago in a flu epidemic. Art, her father, never was much good with money. About six months ago I heard that he was accused by the general store owner of stealing small items from the store where he worked.

"No charges were ever filed but Art lost his job. The family's been hard put since then. I'm surprised that the girl would admit to something like this. Thought we better come over and have a talk with her and her father."

They went up and knocked on the door. A young girl answered. She had on a much washed dress a size too small for her and her hair was uncombed.

"Opal?" Mitzi asked. "Is that you? I'm Mitzi Roland. I used to know you when we were both going to Central School."

A flicker of recognition flashed over the girl's face. She nodded. "I remember you. You always had pretty dresses."

"May we come in? This is my friend, Mr. Morgan."

"My pa ain't here. He's out looking for work."

"We need to talk to you, Opal. It's important."

She sighed and nodded. Inside the living room was a jumble of homemade furniture that needed a good cleaning. They sat on benches and Mitzi went right to the point.

"Opal, you told your father that Mr. Blackhawk accosted you. I know Harry Blackhawk. He's a kind and gentle person. I don't think he did anything to you."

"Yes he did. Just what I told the sheriff." She crossed her arms in front of her and a defiant look came over her face. "He did too. I said so, and he can't deny it."

"He has denied it, Opal. It's just your word against his."

"He did it. Just like my Daddy told me to tell them." Her eyes went wide a minute and her hand flashed up to cover her face.

Mitzi smiled. "So your father told you to say that Mr. Blackhawk molested you. That's what you just said, Opal."

"No, no. I told Daddy what he did. Then he talked to the sheriff and then I told the sheriff what Blackhawk did to me twice."

"The charges say it was three times. Was it twice or three times, Opal?"

"Yes, three times."

"Did your Daddy tell you to say that it was three times?"

"Yes. No. I told Daddy." Opal covered her face with both hands. Tears seeped between her fingers, and she began to sob.

"Opal, I don't believe you even know who Harry Blackhawk is, do you? I don't believe that he ever touched you or looked at you strange or spoke to you. He isn't that kind of a man. He was a favorite of my father's and I've known him for ten years. He's always been polite and a gentleman."

"He's a heathen, an Indian. Don't matter what happens to him."

"Is that what your father told you to say? Did your father tell you that when he made you lie to the sheriff?"

"Daddy told me he was an Indian."

"Would you know who Blackhawk was if you saw him on the street, Opal?"

"Well, I guess so. Sure. But it was dark when he touched me."

"Then how did you know it was him?"

"They told me."

"Your father and the sheriff?"

The tears came again. Then she sobbed and leaned into Mitzi's arms.

"I didn't want to do it. I told my pa I was sorry and I wouldn't let the Benoit boy touch me any more. I was just curious and he caught us and he pounded on the Benoit boy and chased him home and screamed and yelled at his pa. Then he came back and asked me did the boy . . . you know." She looked at Buckskin. "Did he do it to me, and I said no.

"Then just a week later, yesterday, pa told me he'd been talking with the sheriff and Mr. Ingles, he owns the store. Pa told me what to say. Said I had to do it. Just no way around it. If I didn't we'd both get in a lot of trouble."

They heard sounds from the front door and a man came into the room quickly.

He was slender, had on a coat and tie and a dingy white shirt. He had shaved but not too well.

"Who are you people in my house?" he demanded.

Mitzi stood and held out her hand. "I'm Mitzi Roland. I own the Box R Ranch and I want to help you and Opal."

"We don't need nobody to help us. I got me a chance of a job. I used to be a cook back in Iowa. Got me a chance to work four hours a day down at the Boise cafe. Not sure yet."

"Opal said the sheriff and you talked to her about Harry Blackhawk. Why was the sheriff with you? Did you get in trouble stealing again?"

Arthur Denley's face flared red and he shouted something that Mitzi didn't understand. He turned around and marched away from them muttering and raving. When he came back he had calmed himself.

"You always mess in other folks business this way?"

"When your business puts a friend of mine in danger, I certainly do mess with them. You've falsely charged Harry Blackhawk with a serious crime. He could be sent to prison for thirty years, do you realize that?"

"Thirty years? The sheriff said he'd get maybe six months on the county work crew on the road."

"The sheriff said that?"

"Yeah. Said it was about time that somebody—" Denley stopped. His shoulders sagged and he sat down heavily on a chair and rubbed his face.

"What's a man supposed to do? I try to take care of my daughter. She don't have no good clothes to go to school in. She don't have no friends. Then I lose my job and we don't have half enough to eat.

"All right, so I tried to steal some bread and cheese from old Ingles at the store. He catches me and takes me over to the sheriff's office demanding that he do something about it. The sheriff talked with Ingles, gave him twenty dollars and he went away happy.

"Then he looks at me and says I can square things with him easy. All I have to do is swear that Harry Blackhawk molested my daughter, three times. Easy. I sign the complaint, we tell Opal what to say and we stuff this Indian saddlemaker in the hoosegow. He also gave me ten dollars to buy food with. I bought food, I'm not a drinker."

Mitzi looked at the broken man. All he needed was a good job. She made up her mind at once. "Mr. Denley, how would you like a permanent job at my ranch as my cook? We only have eight hands, but with you and me and Opal that would make eleven of us. Twelve for a while. I'll pay you thirty dollars a month and found. You and Opal can have rooms in the ranch house. Plenty of room. I need a cook."

"Well, I don't know. Move way out there?"

"The move will do you good. What do you say?"

"What do I have to do to get this good job?"

"All you have to do is to tell the District Attorney exactly what you told me. I think we can convince the DA to drop all charges against Harry Blackhawk and he won't file any complaints against you or Opal. Is it a deal?"

A half hour later, the four of them walked into the District Attorney's office and got an immediate hearing. Neal Varick had been doing some soul searching of his own. He'd heard about the sheriff's sneaky try to swindle the Box R Ranch away from Mitzi.

Now he listened with amazement as Art Denley told his story. He made rapid notes on a yellow pad of paper. When Art finished, he looked at the DA who was still writing. Art glanced quickly at Mitzi and Buckskin. They both nodded.

A moment later the DA grinned. "All right. Now I'll want to go over this again with Mr. Denley, but I think I have the gist of it. To me it looks like the only law that has been broken here has been done by Sheriff Lombard.

"I'll withdraw all charges against Harry Blackhawk at once and have him released. Just as soon as I can today, I'll draw up charges against Isaiah Lombard of bribery and blackmail and enticing an underage person to file a false police report. These felony charges will be presented to the Territorial Attorney General who will be the one to prosecute the charges."

The DA grinned. "I know for a fact that the sheriff is out at his ranch. Be there today and tomorrow. I'll carry the orders over right now to the jail to release Blackhawk with the county's apologies."

The four trooped out of the courthouse and stood a moment looking at each other. Mitzi took the lead.

"Will we need a wagon to haul your goods out to my ranch, Mr. Denley?"

"You want us to come out, right away?"

"Right now would be fine. A wagon?"

"Oh land sakes, not a big one. We rent the house and our furniture ain't much. You seen it. A small wagon would be plenty."

Buckskin nodded and turned toward his horse. "I'll get one and bring it by. You three can go and pack up."

Buckskin rented a wagon at the livery, and stopped by the saddle shop. Blackhawk already was working at the saddle he had on his bench.

He grinned when he saw Buckskin. "Seems like you been busy."

"Just mending a little bit of fencing. You get to stay overnight with the county?"

"About the size of it. Charges all dropped. Thanks."

"You owe me a trail cooked dinner one of these nights."

"Done."

Buckskin told Blackhawk about the new cook out at the ranch.

The big Indian laughed. "He goes from bad guy to cook all in sight of an hour. That Mitzi has a way about her, doesn't she?"

"A right nice way, and a good lady to have for a friend." He headed for the door. "I better get this wagon on over to the house. Moving day. Check on you later."

The move went well. Art Denley and Opal put their things together within an hour and before three o'clock they pulled the wagon into the Box R Ranch.

Jody saw them coming and rode out to meet them.

"Been hoping you'd be back early. How is Blackhawk?"

They told him and he grinned.

"That's good news. Wish I had good news. I don't. I just got back from the south range near the river. I came on fifteen head of branded Black Kettle steers and cows. All of them were so lame they could hardly walk and had drooling and ulcers in their mouths. Sure as rain looks like hoof and mouth disease. If it is, it could wipe out our whole herd in a month."

Buckskin scowled. "Get together every hand you can find. Bring rifles, and five gallon cans of coal oil and shovels. We got some tough work to do and we've got to do it in a rush."

Chapter Ten

The diseased cattle were about an hour away from the ranch buildings. They made good time. When they came on them, Buckskin could pick out the sick ones in a glance. They were well distributed among the healthy cattle, which wasn't a pleasant sight. That would take extra work.

Buckskin rode close to one brood cow that was down on her front knees. She couldn't stand on her front legs. They were a mass of sores. She drooled and he could see sores on her mouth. He took his six-gun and shot her in the head from two feet away as her big brown eyes looked up at him in pain and wonder.

"Drive our stock away from the sick ones," Buckskin shouted. "Then we'll shoot these diseased ones. Get moving, minutes could count on this."

It took them twenty minutes to get fifty head

of their own stock moved away from the sick animals. Then the slaughter began. They formed a line with their rifles and rode forward and killed the sick animals as they rode up to them, putting them out of their misery.

Jody rode over to Buckskin with a questioning look. "What happens now?"

"Use the coal oil. Douse each animal well and then set them all on fire. We might be able to contain that bug that's causing the sickness, whatever it is. Be careful not to touch any of the sores or the animals at all if you can help it."

The fifteen fires burned brightly until the coal oil was consumed. The hair had burned off and the tail and ears and the sickening smell of the burning hair and hide made two of the men violently ill. They saw that not much of the animals had burned up and now lay there smoking. They threw on the rest of the coal oil and lit them again. When that burned out there still hadn't been much of the carcass that had been burned. Buckskin shrugged.

"Best we can do. Now with the shovels. We need a foot of dirt over every carcass."

That was the work part of the job. It was dusk before they had shoveled the soil and sod and weeds over the dead cattle. When they were done, they stood beside their horses breathing hard and wiping at honest sweat.

Buckskin had done his share of shoveling.

"Good work, men. Now let's get these live ones in a herd and move them away from the other animals."

"Going to quarantine them for a while?" Jody asked.

"That's the idea. If they come down with hoof and mouth we don't want them mixed with the rest of the herd."

"I know a box canyon about four miles from here where we could string a couple of strands of barbed wire and keep them in."

Buckskin grinned. "Fine idea, Jody. You're starting to earn your pay. Let's move this bunch out in that direction. Oh, you better send two men back to the ranch to bring a wagon with posts and wire and pliers and staples and hammers so we can string that fence. It'll be night work, but it could save the rest of the herd."

They came to the valley in the edge of the mountains about an hour later. There was plenty of room for the fifty head of steers, yearlings, and brood cows and lots of grass. Buckskin and Jody sized up the place in the dark and figured where the fence should go. It would be just under one-hundred yards across the mouth of the valley. It widened considerably behind that which made it ideal.

The wagon got there a little after nine in the evening, and the three fresh hands who came along were put to work with two post hole diggers making the ten holes they'd need for the posts. The pine posts had been split out of ponderosa pine weeks before and had cured out well.

At that time they had been also cut to length, about seven feet long. That way they could be dug into the ground three feet deep and four feet of post would remain above ground. They wouldn't last more than a few years, but for now they would work fine.

By ten o'clock, they had the post holes dug and

two men came along behind the diggers setting in the posts and filling in dirt around them and tamping them in solid and straight. Two men came behind them with the roll of barbed wire. They strung one strand two feet off the ground out to the first five posts.

There they cut it off and put on the next strand at three feet back the other way. The barbed wire went on the posts with two-inch long staples that held it fast.

When the other posts were in and solid, the wire men followed. By eleven o'clock they had the fence up and finished.

Jody began to laugh. The falling down tired men stared at him in surprise.

"We forgot to put in a gate," Jody howled. To get the critters out of there we'll have to cut the wire."

The weary men nodded at Jody and mounted up and headed with the wagon back to the ranch. One man went to sleep on the ride and nearly fell off his mount. They made it to the ranch a little after one o'clock in the morning and all dropped into their bunks asleep before they could get their boots off.

Most of the men didn't get up for breakfast. They slept until nine o'clock and then staggered out, still tired. Buckskin had the new cook do a quick breakfast for the men and he talked with Mitzi.

"While it was still light, we could see a few tracks. Looked like the fifteen head had been deliberately driven into your range, and into a scattering of cattle."

"The sick cattle had to come from the Black

Kettle," Mitzi said. "You said they carried the B bar K brand. This is the worst thing Lombard has ever done. If that hoof and mouth disease gets going, I've heard it can sweep through an entire section of the country killing hundreds of thousands of animals."

"I've seen it wipe out one big spread in two months," Buckskin said. "In this case, I think we've got it contained. We'll send one man out to check on those penned in cattle every day. If any of them are down, we'll drag them out, shoot them and bury them."

"How long does it take for the disease to show up in other cattle?" Mitzi asked.

"I don't know for sure. I've heard some cattlemen say it takes about a month."

"So what kind of retaliation are you planning?"

"None. I'd say it's time to pull back and let the law take care of Lombard. The Attorney General is after him on those bribery charges. I'm sure the DA will send that through the Attorney General. Then the DA has pushed the bribery, blackmail and forcing an underage girl to file a false police report on those charges against Blackhawk. All of this done under the color of authority.

"If he gets prosecuted on either one fairly, he should go to prison for a long, long time."

They heard some commotion outside and they went out the kitchen door and saw Blackhawk ride into the ranch, bareback as usual with only a thin saddle blanket between him and the horse. The big sturdy paint turned toward them with no apparent direction by Blackhawk.

The big Indian wore only a leather vest over

Kit Dalton

his brawny shoulders and chest and a pair of jeans. He stepped down from his mount, left it ground tied and walked up to Mitzi and Buckskin.

"Things happening in town," Blackhawk said. He sniffed. "That coffee smells about ready. Could a weary redskin have a cup?"

Inside they poured cups around and had oatmeal cookies the new cook had come up with. Then Blackhawk got down to the important news.

"This morning the Attorney General took over the Ada county sheriff's office in Boise. Lombard has been suspended from his duties as sheriff and a six-man team from the Territorial government will do the work there until Lombard is cleared of all charges, or he's convicted and a new sheriff is elected."

"Hooray!" Mitzi shouted. She put her arms around Blackhawk and hugged him. "You bring the best kind of news."

"He's been charged with jury tampering, four counts, and bribery, four counts, and also charged with blackmail and forcing an underage person to make a false statement to police all under the color of authority."

Mitzi frowned. "Color of authority. What does that mean?"

"He did it while he was sheriff and using that authority to help him commit his criminal acts," Buckskin said.

Mitzi laughed. "Good, I think we've got him at last."

"Maybe not," Blackhawk said. The Attorney General's men can't find Isaiah Lombard. He's not in his town house or at his ranch."

"He's around somewhere," Buckskin said. "Just wonder what he's thinking about now."

"He's plotting how to get revenge on the three of us," Blackhawk said. "We've been the ones who caused all his troubles."

Buckskin nodded. "Meaning he'll be coming after us with all the firepower he has left. Where are our cowhands?"

Mitzi frowned. "Three are finishing driving about three-hundred head of cows and calves up to the north mesa. We decided to move the herd up to the higher country by stages. They should be back by noon.

"Four of them are working the south pasture looking for strays, doctoring any more black leg they find. Jody rode over to check on the hoof and mouth disease pen."

"We better get everyone back we can," Buckskin said. "If I don't miss my guess, we're going to have visitors with guns. Lots of visitors. I'd say we better start getting ready. When will Jody be back?"

"He'll be back in half an hour," Mitzi said.

"Want to be in our army?" Buckskin asked Blackhawk.

He nodded.

"Good. You will be our first lookout. Get to the top of the barn roof. There's a way up from the shed in back and a ladder. Perch up there and watch for any dust trails coming our way. You'll be able to see up any dust trail before any of us white men can."

Buckskin went to the kitchen door and picked up a Henry repeating rifle and tossed it to the

Indian. "Might come in handy."

Ten minutes later four riders came in from the south range. Buckskin met them, asked if they had seen anything unusual. They said no. He told them about the war party he figured was on the way. They dug out their rifles, boxes of rounds and checked their six-guns. The three riders came in from the north mesa a few minutes after that.

A half hour later, just before noon, Jody came riding in at a gallop. His horse was foam flecked and wild eyed as Jody pulled up when he saw Buckskin.

"We got trouble," Jody said. "After I checked the penned animals I swung around toward the north mesa to see how the animals up there were taking to their new home. I saw our riders far off heading back to the barn after they finished the short drive. Then I saw some more riders. They were at the far end of the herd and seemed to be gathering them, herding them into a pack. Then they began to move the animals forward toward the cliff."

"Must be Lombard's men," Buckskin said. "How far is it up there?"

"Two miles," Jody said.

"Have we got time to get there?"

"They were still gathering. I figured it would take them two hours to get the herd put into place before they try to drive them over the cliff."

"Let's go. Every man get a rifle and mount up," Buckskin bellowed. "Blackhawk, come on down, we need you." Buckskin made a quick stop in the barn and took something out of a box that he put in his saddlebags.

138

Ten of them thundered out of the ranch yard five minutes later. Mitzi watched them go. Buckskin had yelled at her when she said she wanted to go along.

"Absolutely not. There could be a lot of shooting. We need you to stay here and watch for riders coming this way."

The riders galloped for half a mile, then slowed their mounts for a walking rest, then galloped again. They came around the edge of the slope up to the plateau in about forty-five minutes. They could see the herd of cows and calves. They were a half mile from the lip of the two-hundred-foot dropoff cliff.

"Get between them and the cliff," Buckskin bellowed.

Now as he rode, he took dynamite sticks from his saddlebags and pushed detonator caps onto them, then inserted four-inch burnable fuses into the hollow end of the dynamite caps. He made ten of the small bombs, then heard a rumble.

At the same time he heard shots from the far end of the herd of cattle. A stampede. The Black Kettle riders had started it.

He rode toward the cattle, lighting and throwing the dynamite sticks as he charged the herd. Fifteen seconds after lighting the first fuse, the dynamite stick exploded. It had no effect on the cattle. Then the others went off, two, then three then four, five, six, seven, eight.

As the explosions caught their attention, the lead cows shied away to the left. He threw the last two sticks of dynamite and saw the rest of the crew riding close to the cattle waving their hats and shouting.

Slowly the front of the herd veered farther to the left, then to the left again until they were running in the form of a giant U, heading back the way they had come.

He heard a shout of pain and then a scream. A cowboy from the Black Kettle Ranch had become lost in the dust as he followed the herd. He blundered out of the dust of the cattle choking and trying to wipe his eyes, just as the lead cows that had brought the herd into a U-turn thundered down on him.

He tried to outrun them to the side, but they had an angle he couldn't overcome. If he'd headed straight ahead of them he could have outdistanced them, but he became confused by the dust and the bawling and the shouts.

A big tan cow with sharp horns hit his horse midsection and pushed it aside where two more cows thundered into it, knocking the horse off its feet and unseating the rider. He went down in a fury of pounding sharp hooves and deadly horns. He screamed once more, then there was no more sound as the stampeding hooves slashed at him as they rushed past.

Buckskin helped shy the last of the strays back the way they had come and away from the cliff. Then he looked at the six cowboys a quarter-of-a-mile away. He pulled his rifle and sent a shot in their direction. The five turned their horses and showed flying tails as they rushed away out of rifle range in the general direction of the Black Kettle range.

Buckskin moved slowly over the heavily trod path of the stampede looking for the downed cowboy. He was easy to find. His horse had died as well when it went down in front of those heavy brood cows and their calves. The horse had a caved in belly and lay on her back with all four feet in the air.

The cowboy was sprawled twenty feet farther on. His face was gone, his belly punched with more than a dozen bloody holes evidently made by sharp hooves. One arm was missing.

The five riders sat on their horses around the body staring at it. Then they turned and moved forward, urging the cattle to walk farther away from the deadly dropoff and to get back to their job of munching on the grass and providing milk for their young calves.

Buckskin counted five dead calves across the stampede route. He saw several brood cows bawling and wandering around through the herd looking for their missing issue.

The men sat on their mounts looking at the now peacefully grazing beef cattle. It seemed that the men were in no rush to leave them.

"I want one man to stay up here until dark to guard these critters," Buckskin said.

One of the new men held up his hand. "Might as well be me. I don't want to see them animals going over the side."

Back at the ranch, they stabled their mounts, rubbed them down and then put them in the corral.

"I want three horses kept saddled at all times for the next few days," Buckskin said. "Want somebody who can move fast if we need to set up a little counterattack."

One man was assigned to perch on the barn roof shortly after they rode in. Mitzi suggested where some of the other riders could wait in various spots around the ranch buildings, all with rifles and extra ammunition.

"Nothing else doing here," Mitzi told Buckskin after he reported that the brood cows and all but five of the calves were safe. He gave her a recounting of the attack and the turning of the herd.

"What made you think of dynamite?" Mitzi asked.

"I've seen it done before to start a stampede. Figured it might work just as well to stop one. The dynamite sits right there in the barn so I knew where to find the makings."

"Think Lombard is through?" Mitzi asked.

Buckskin shook his head. "Not by a damn sight. He'll fight us and fight us until he wins it all or loses it all. He knows now that he won't be able to win in court. The people he used to be able to scare and tell what to do, aren't frightened of him anymore. He must figure that since he can't do it in the court, he'll try for both spreads and hole up here like a hermit hoping the world will pass him by."

"But it won't."

Supper that night was served in shifts, with four men watching in their selected defensive positions. They did four hours on, then slept four hours. By midnight Buckskin decided it was going to work. He saw the lamp still burning in the kitchen. He went up and knocked on the door.

Mitzi sat there in a robe with a shotgun on the table and sipping at a cup of coffee.

"Your shift over?" she asked as he came in at her call.

"Yes."

"Good, have some coffee." She poured a cup from the cooling pot on the long plank table. "Is this all ever going to end?"

"Soon, maybe sooner than we expect. The Attorney General's men will catch Lombard, or we'll find him and maybe do the job ourselves."

"I don't think he'll attack us tonight," Mitzi said. "He lost one man in that stampede try. His soldiers aren't going to be so quick to volunteer to go out to a shooting war again."

"Probably right. I hope so."

"Then there's tomorrow. My guess is that if he comes, it'll be tomorrow."

"Until then we all need to get some sleep."

"True. Buckskin, you know you told me I should pick out a nice young man and get married."

"I said that, yes."

"I've picked him out. Jody. I'm going to marry Jody. He knows the business, knows this ranch. We'll be partners on it. I've told him how I feel. He's getting used to the idea. A couple of more talks with him and some heavy kissing and I think he'll be convinced."

"Good." He stood up. "I better get some sleep."

"Me, too. Walk me down to my room. You carry the lamp."

He took the coal oil lamp and they walked out of the kitchen to the hallway. As they went he watched her discarding the robe, then her nightgown and as they came to her bedroom door, she turned to him, naked and smiling.

"Buckskin Morgan. This time you can't turn me

down. I don't want to go to my honeymoon bed a virgin. I want to be able to satisfy Jody every way I can. I want you to teach me exactly how to do that, all of it. Right now. I simply won't take no for an answer."

Chapter Eleven

Buckskin looked at the naked form of Mitzi standing in front of him. Perfect, young breasts so full. A slender waist, flaring hips and delicious legs tapering to bare feet.

"Buckskin, nobody but you has ever seen me naked before. I've saved it all for you." She reached up and kissed him, then let him go and with her hands behind his head, pulled him down so his face was in front of her breasts. She pushed one up to his mouth which he slowly opened, then nibbled on her and sucked her tender white flesh deep into his mouth.

"Oh, yes, Buckskin. Now that's the spirit." She lifted him away. "Come into my bedroom before we burn the place down by dropping the lamp. I want three lamps lit so I can see every square inch of you naked and making love to me."

Inside her bedroom she had already closed the

shutters. One lamp was burning. She had him set down the second, then lit a third and put it on a chair near the bed.

She caught his hands and put them over her breasts.

"First, a question. Why do men like girl's breasts so much? I've seen boys get all tongue-tied and stare at my breasts and then run away. One boy touched my breast through my dress once and he groaned and humped his hips against me. Why do men like breasts?"

They sat down on the bed and he caressed her breasts, bent and kissed them, then took a long breath. "Breasts. Men like to call them tits. It's because a woman's breasts are the easiest part of a woman's sexual equipment to see. They stand right out there on her chest, poking at him, touching him sometimes when he gets a hug, bold and beautiful and so enticing.

"A young boy dreams of touching a girl's breasts, then of seeing one all bare. Breasts are usually the first thing a man looks at when he sees a woman. It doesn't matter if they are huge, or tiny or somewhere in between. Just the idea of seeing and touching a woman's bare breasts gets most men all worked up in about three seconds."

"I still don't understand. My breasts are just another part of me, like my elbows. Do they excite you?"

"Mitzi, do you look at the bulge in a man's pants behind his fly?"

She put her hands over her face, and moved them slowly as she nodded. "Yes, I admit I do. I wonder what a man looks like."

"That's about the same way a man reacts to a woman's breasts."

She put her hands down and touched the hardness behind his fly. "I still wonder what a man looks like." She looked up at him with a questioning smile.

"Help yourself, take a look. Remember to be gentle because he's going to mean a lot to you pretty soon."

Mitzi shivered as she unbuttoned the fasteners on his fly. She looked up at him once and he nodded. She opened his belt and spread back his pants.

"Underwear." Mitzi glanced up at him and giggled. "I didn't know that men wore underwear."

"Most of us do. Simply warmer in winter and more comfortable in summer."

His short underwear bulged where his erection tented it out. All in a rush she lifted his underwear at the waist and pulled it out and down. His erection sprang up.

"Oh!" she said, surprised. Her eyes widened and her mouth came open in wonder. Then she moved closer and bent to look at him without touching him.

"So big, so long, so. . . . Oh my. I've had my finger in. . . . I don't see how he could ever get inside my—"

"Touch him, he won't break, at least not easily. Go ahead, give it a try."

She touched him, then her hand wrapped around him and she grinned. "He's warm."

"The way your breasts are warm."

She urged him to sit up farther on the bed, then investigated his scrotum and his crotch.

147

"So much hair," she said to herself. She looked up with a small frown. "But he's not that way all the time?"

"No, just when a beautiful girl undresses in front of me. The reaction is quite swift."

"How does he look when he's not all hard that way?"

"You'll have to wait and see."

She looked at him. "Oh, you mean after-wards. . . . after we do it and he spurts, then he goes all limp?"

"You're learning fast. I had a doctor friend who calls that limp time the refractory period. The time needed after an ejaculation before he'll get hard again."

Mitzi nodded but he doubted she heard much of what he said. She had gripped his shaft again and stroked down on the loose skin, then back up.

"I heard a word, masturbate. Is that what this would be? You know, if I kept it up until you shoot?"

"You know a lot you haven't told me. Yes. That would be masturbation. Where did you hear that?"

"At school two years ago. An older girl was talking one day and touching herself. She said she did it almost every night, to herself, but she still hadn't done it with a boy."

She looked at him and suddenly bent and kissed the head of his penis. It bucked in delight and she kissed it again, then edged away. She watched him a moment and he could hear her breathing quicken.

"Please help me undress you. I want you as

bare as I am right now. Please hurry!"

She pulled off his boots and then his pants and his underwear. He did his leather vest and his shirt. Then they lay side by side on the bed with her arms around him, her breasts pushed hard against his chest.

"Now I'm getting scared," she said, her mouth pressed hard against his neck.

"Why?"

"I've never been naked in bed before with a handsome man who I've told I want him to fuck me."

She looked up at him when she said the "f" word out loud for the first time in her life. Then she giggled.

"Say it again, you won't be so afraid. Nothing to worry about. The first time to find out about making love has to come for you. I'll take it as slow and gentle and easy as you want me to. If you decide that tonight is not the right time, we'll stop. No problems, no regrets. Understood?"

She nodded and reached down and held his erection.

"I just don't see how something that . . . that huge . . . can ever penetrate my little cunnie."

"Have you ever seen a baby born?"

She shook her head. "No . . . oh, I see."

"You ladies have the great ability called dilation. The muscles and tissue down there can expand and expand and expand until it's eight or nine inches across, larger yet so the baby can come through."

She nodded. "Yes, I understand."

"Now, take a look down there. If a newborn baby can come out, do you think there'll be any problem with junior down there making his way inside?"

"Oh, Lord, I never thought of it that way."

"When you get in the right mood, you'll get all warm and wet down there and already you'll start to expand. There won't be any trouble at all."

"Hold me, Buckskin. Just hold me."

He held her tight. Soon she squirmed and her hands went back to his waist and caught him. Slowly she turned over on her back.

"Pet my titties, they need attention. Caress them and then kiss them and bite them. I want you to seduce me tonight. It might take a while, but we've got until morning."

He stroked her breasts, fondled them, warmed them, then kissed them. She caught one of his hands and put it down to her crotch. Her legs were tightly together. He worked his hand down to her knee and pushed her legs apart. She moaned gently as he did, the kissed his lips long and hard.

Buckskin brought his hand up her soft, inner thigh and she wailed low. His fingers brushed across her wet center and she gasped, then pushed his fingers back to the delicate spot.

"Touch me there, Morgan. Touch me!"

He brushed her outer lips, caressing them, stroking them, then dipping in gently to her heartland with a finger. She moaned again and humped her hips toward him.

His finger moved higher to the hard node just below her pubis and he hit it. Her eyes went wide and she gasped. He strummed her clit twice more and she looked at him.

"That's what the girl in school meant about doing happy fingers almost every night?"

He nodded, then kissed her and strummed her node again and again. She yelped, then brayed softly and tore into a climax that made the one the night before seem like a foothill to this mountain peak.

Her whole body shook like it had a million nerve endings set on fire. She humped and shook and rattled and her body pounded against him. Her mouth opened but no sound came out. Her eyes closed and she almost finished one climax when a second one shot through her.

"Oh damn, oh damn, oh damn. Oh! Oh! Oh! Yes, yes, yes, yes. I think I'm gonna die! Yes, I love it. Love it. Love it. Oh, sweet Buckskin, wonderful. Again, again, again!"

He touched her clit again and she charged off into another long series of vibrations and spasms and moans and chattering little meaningless phrases that tore her apart and at last dropped her back on the bed so limp she could do little but open her eyes a moment and look at him, then close them.

It was three or four minutes before she stirred. She looked up at him and that billion dollar smile came across her face. It almost made Buckskin think of settling down. Almost.

"Buckskin Morgan, you just tear me apart, you know that? I've never felt that way before. Never in my long life."

He grinned. "It gets better. Give me your hand." She did and he put it on his erection. "Let's find a warm home for this weary traveler."

"Now, right now?"

"Yes, you're ready. Right now."

She rolled to her back and spread her legs, then lifted her knees and helped him come between her thighs. She held his erection and urged him forward until the tip of him touched her crotch. She adjusted him and then guided him to her heartland.

"Right there," she said softly.

He knew she was wet and ready. He probed gently and entered her an inch or so. She gasped and then smiled.

"Nothing like I've ever felt before. You're right, there is room."

He waited a moment, then pushed in a little farther. Her lubricant coated him and then he slid all the way home and Mitzi gasped and clasped her arms around his back and kissed his shoulder and whatever else she could reach.

"Yes, yes!" she crooned. "I . . . I can't describe it. Oh, yes! I want you there always."

Her hips pushed up, fell away, then pushed up again.

He looked at her. "Why did you do that?"

"With my hips? I wanted more of you inside, then slip out and come back in. It just felt like the right thing to do."

He kissed her. "It is."

The basic move of lovemaking but nobody had to teach her or instruct her. It was part of the basic human knowledge.

He growled softly. "My turn." He drove into her hard and heard her gasp. Then he plowed ahead again and she came upward to meet him.

They set up a system and before long he was panting and panting. He felt the gates high upstream open and the flood storm down through his tubes.

The sky fell and the moon and stars exploded and all sorts of shooting stars blazed across the heavens. He felt her surge into another climax even as he was in the middle of his and they both panted and moaned. She wailed loud and long and then stopped and he gave one final burst and fell on her, dead to the universe for a few minutes.

When he recovered, he rolled away from her and stared down.

"Now, young lady. You've had your first love-making experience. You're no longer a virgin. You can take your young man to bed and know more than he does about sex. I'd bet a bucket of gold that Jody is a virgin himself."

"No, there aren't any men virgins."

"Lot of them out there. Most men don't go to the whores. Most young men can't afford them, would be too embarrassed to try it anyway. Boys talk big, but most of them are just big talkers."

She reached over and kissed him. "I feel so delicious. I feel like I'm capable of doing anything right now. That the whole world is mine and I can go and do and be whatever I decide. I've never felt this way before."

"That's the best part of making love. It has a tremendous binding effect, a big reason you should keep your bedding to one man and only one man. After tonight, that is."

She smiled. "Now, how are we going to do it next? My friend said there are several positions such as me on top, on the side, even on hands and knees."

Buckskin grinned. "Just once isn't enough for you to savor?"

"Oh, no. At least four times, all different ways, so I'll be able to help Jody."

In a few minutes he was ready again. His refractory period was shorter today than sometimes.

"Get on your hands and knees," he told her.

"You're joking. We can do it the way the dogs and animals do?"

"Just wait and see, young lady."

She moved on her hands and knees and he spread her knees apart a little and got on his knees behind her. She turned and looked over her shoulder.

"This can really work?"

"It can work." He moved up close to her and then probed gently to find the right slot. She yelped when he probed and slid into her.

"I never would have believed it," she said softly. "But oh, that's the wildest sensation. Much different from before. Better even."

He reached under her and caught both her hanging breasts with his hands and began a slow series of thrusts. Before the first six or eight were over he felt her climax roaring down on them. He couldn't match it. He let her jolt through her satisfaction and helped her along a little, then as she trailed off after four hard climaxes, he drove into her harder. His hands came away from her breasts and caught the front of her hips for leverage and then jolted hard at her until he exploded in one series of hammer blows that drove her forward until her arms collapsed and she fell on her shoulders on the bed.

He finished and she wailed in delight. They lay

154

there on the bed that way for a few minutes, then he moved off her and she rolled over and kissed him.

"Now that was different, and a little strange. But it didn't hurt. I loved it. Now I let you rest a few minutes and then we have at least three more times."

She was partly right. In the end they both fell asleep after the third time and didn't wake up until the roosters crowed in the chicken house at sunrise the next morning.

After breakfast, Buckskin sent Jody into town in the small rig to bring back coal oil, another ball of barbed wire, more blackleg salve and some food stuffs the cook requested.

None of the lookouts reported anything unusual around the ranch buildings the previous night. Buckskin let half of them get in another four hours of sleep, and set the others to ranch duties. One of the old hands who knew where the hoof and mouth disease animals were penned, was sent over to make the daily check on them.

Buckskin rode out half a mile to the south generally toward the Black Kettle Ranch and sat on his horse looking toward the other outfit. Lombard must be down there gathering his forces. He lost one man on the stampede, but that wouldn't slow him down. It might cause him some problems in getting his cowhands to be gunhands, but for that he'd have to wait and see.

Buckskin figured without fail that Lombard would make one last ditch try to do in the people who had hurt him. That was Blackhawk, Buckskin and the whole Box R. He'd be coming, but would it be in the daylight or the dark?

After a half hour of watching, Buckskin turned and rode back to the ranch. They had sent Jody out early that morning and by noon he was back with three copies of the local newspaper, *The Ada County Recorder*.

On the front page were two lead stories. The top headline blared: Sheriff Lombard Booted. The story told how the Territorial Attorney General had relieved the county sheriff of his duties, charged him with eight felony counts and put out three warrants for his arrest on the charges.

It told how the sheriff hadn't been in his county office for the past two days, and that the six men from the Attorney General's office were handling the routine duties of the sheriff's department and taking care of lawbreakers as well.

"There has been no breakdown in law enforcement in Ada county," Attorney General Floyd Perkins said. "Men from my territorial department have the situation well in hand and we will assist the current deputies in running the county's law business until Isaiah Lombard is tried and acquitted on all charges, or he is convicted, and a new sheriff is elected by the citizens of Ada county."

In another story the charges were detailed. The smaller headline proclaimed: Lombard Faces Eight Felony Counts. The story listed the charges against Lombard for the jury bribery, for false accusations, for bribery of a citizen, for enticing a citizen to file a false police report in the case of the Harry Blackhawk charges which were filed last week and quickly voided.

A smaller story indicated that a separate charge had been filed by the Attorney General against

Lombard for issuing an illegal wanted poster without having proper court authorization and court supplied warrants of an actual crime having been committed.

"The then sheriff put Buckskin Lee Morgan in dire danger of being shot down in response to the wanted posters," the news story stated. "Several confrontations were reported and at least one death resulted from such confrontations, the nature of which was ruled to be self-defense."

Another story at the bottom of the front page reported that Slash Wade, part-time deputy sheriff, was found shot to death a mile south of town along the railroad right of way. A train employee saw the body and a sheriff's deputy retrieved it.

Blackhawk had ridden back with Jody. He shook Buckskin's hand and grinned. "Figure you should have somebody out here who knows about attacks by white-eyes on poor, innocent folks."

Buckskin and Blackhawk took a walk around the ranch yard and when they came back they had a defense of sorts worked out. One man was put on top of the barn as a 360-degree lookout. One mounted man was sent a half mile to the south, another one a half mile to the east, as mobile lookouts.

"You see any dust trails coming our way, you turn tail and get back here fast as you can," Buckskin told the two mounted men. They nodded and rode off, rifles and six-guns all loaded.

Buckskin and Blackhawk had missed dinner. They went in and had a solid meal of meat and potatoes from the new cook. Buckskin waved at Denley and thanked him for the fine meal. His daughter was in the kitchen helping him and her smile was as wide as her father's.

Mitzi sat down with the two men and asked what they figured was going to happen.

"Lombard will attack us today or tonight just after dark," Buckskin said. "No hard evidence, just a feeling. He's wasted too much time now. There's no place he can run. The train people will report him if he tries to get on one of the passenger runs or even a freight. He's not that good on a horse anymore. I'd guess he'll take one last gasp attack on your ranch just for plain old hatred and revenge."

The hoof and mouth rider came back reporting that he could find no evidence of any of the cattle in the fenced canyon having any symptoms of the disease.

"Let's hope that it stays that way," Mitzi said.

About three o'clock two riders came from the south. The roof lookout reported that the two men stopped and talked with the mounted sentry in that direction, then came on toward the ranch. The lookout stayed in place.

They rode into the ranch yard a few minutes later. One of them was Claude Roland, Mitzi's brother. He stopped short when he saw his sister.

"Mitzi, dear sister. I hear you bought our ranch at the sheriff's sale and beat me out of my half."

She laughed. "No such thing. You still are half owner even if it doesn't say so on the new deed. Any profits are half yours. Now come inside and have some coffee or lemonade or some late dinner."

The other rider spoke up. "Miss Roland. I'm Jeremy Newgate from the Territorial Attorney

General's office. Mr. Perkins just wanted to let you know about the warrants for Isaiah Lombard and to warn you that there is a chance the man might take it in his head to try for some revenge against your ranch."

Mitzi smiled. "Thanks for the warning. You want to stay and man a lookout for us, or would you rather sit here and wait with a good rifle and fifty rounds of ammunition?"

The rider grinned and shook his head. "Afraid I can't do that, but I could use a cup of coffee before I turn around and ride back."

"When you came past the Black Kettle, did you notice any unusual activity?" Buckskin asked.

The messenger shook his head. "It's nigh a half mile over there from the wagon road, but I didn't see no big dust trails or such. We'll just have to wait and hope. Mr. Perkins said we'll give Lombard two more days to give himself up, then we'll take about thirty men and ride out to his ranch and try to talk him into letting us arrest him.

"We figure with thirty rifles aimed at them, about half of his gun-hands will take off out the back side of the barn in a big rush."

Inside the ranch house kitchen, Denley fixed coffee and lemonade, then made big sandwiches for both the riders. Mitzi and her brother talked quietly at one side of the kitchen. He finished his meal and went down the hall to his bedroom to pack some things.

"Well, Claude has decided. He's moving to Chicago. Says he wants to learn about the big city. We've worked out an arrangement. Since I'll be working the ranch, and he won't, he'll get twenty-five percent of the profits. We'll work out a payment twice a year for him. I'm giving him five-hundred dollars which should tide him over for a year even in a big place like Chicago.

"He wants to go on to New York eventually. He'll play it as it comes, he told me."

Somebody yelled outside. Buckskin started for the door. A cowboy burst into the kitchen.

"Wally up on the roof says there's a dust cloud coming at us. Says it's still four or five miles off but it's coming faster than a horse at a walk. Coming up from the south, from the area where the Black Kettle Ranch is."

Chapter Twelve

They all ran into the yard to check on the dust cloud the lookout on the barn had reported coming from the south. They couldn't see it yet.

"Looks like they headed straight for the sentry down there," the lookout from on top called.

The people below waited. Some men checked their rifles. Others levered a round into the firing chamber and some put a sixth bullet in their revolvers.

"How many are there?" Mitzi asked, the strain starting to show on her pretty face.

"Probably can't tell yet," Buckskin said.

Five minutes later the man on top of the barn called out again. "Our lookout down there is racing back this way. He must have seen the dust by now. Maybe he can give us a count."

Buckskin waved at the lookout, then began

placing men in the strategic spots he and Black-hawk had picked out.

Just as the south lookout raced into the ranch yard, they heard a rifle shot and a second later glass breaking in the kitchen window.

"Down everyone!" Buckskin shouted. "The shot came from the north. Lookout, take a look to the north. What can you see?"

The man on the barn gazed that way, checked again and shook his head. "Don't see nothing. There's that gully about six-hundred yards out and then the line of brush along the river. They could have a sniper anywhere along the brushline.

Buckskin sent Mitzi back inside the ranch house by the front door, then got the rest of the men in position.

"Keep a sharp lookout to the south," Buckskin said. "He can't have enough men to attack us from both sides at once. Probably just a sniper up north."

"Couldn't figure out how many riders," the lookout from the south told Buckskin. "From the size of the dust, I'd say at least twenty riders."

The lookout had put his horse in the corral and taken out his rifle and box of shells. Buckskin placed him in the kitchen doorway.

"Flat on your belly with your head behind the casing. You see a target, come around the door and fire, then move back out of danger. Got that?"

The cowhand nodded and ran for his post.

Buckskin went up on the back shed next to the barn. He could see the dust cloud. It had stopped moving forward. The riders were a mile from the ranch buildings. Why the stop? He looked north. He didn't like the north side. Far too much cover up there to make him happy. Lombard could send twenty men with rifles, dynamite and torches down the brush line from the north and they wouldn't see them until they broke out of the brush two-hundred yards from the ranch buildings.

"Keep a sharp look to the north as well," Buckskin called to the rooftop man. He went down and found Blackhawk. He agreed that the brush line was one of their big worries.

"I can go out there and watch up and down the line," Blackhawk said. "If they come that way, they'll most likely walk along the river just outside the brush. Spot them easy."

Buckskin nodded. "Go, but be careful. I want you to make me a new saddle."

The Indian grinned and ran to the north. That was when Buckskin noticed that the Coeur d'Alene wore moccasins. Usually, he wore boots.

Nothing happened for an hour. The afternoon was gone. Dusk began to filter in and devour the daylight. The lookout on the barn top called down one last report.

"The riders where the dust cloud used to be are still just sitting there. Some are off their mounts. They're waiting for something."

Buckskin called for the man to come down and take another position. Buckskin made a round of his men telling them that for sure the raiders would be coming. "They've been waiting for dark," he said. "They'll be coming now. Your first job is to shoot down anyone with a torch. We want to keep the buildings from burning."

He distributed three shotguns and kept one for himself. They were loaded with double-aught buckshot, thirteen balls the size of a .32 round in each of the shells. The double-aught could cut a man in half at fifteen feet.

Buckskin looked to the east. The moon was fuller tonight. As the darkness closed in, the bright moon showed its true light and he found he could see for fifty or sixty feet. One big problem was how to identify the attackers in the darkness?

He made another round telling the men that the first wave of the attack would be by the mounted men. Anyone on a horse was an attacker and fair game.

Then they waited.

An hour into darkness, Buckskin heard two calls from a hoot owl to the north. That was Blackhawk and the call he would make if everything was quiet. Good.

Buckskin made another round of his shooters. "No talking from now on. If you see a bunch of horsemen charging in, fire at the mass of them as soon as you can make them out. A couple of good volleys might discourage some of them. Shoot at the horses or the men, either one will be good targets."

After another hour of no attack, Mitzi came to where Buckskin crouched behind the well.

"Why don't they attack?" she asked.

"It's a good tactic. The defensive people have to be on the alert all the time. The attackers can pick their time and place and rest up and be fresh for the assault. That might be the case or they may be waiting for orders from Lombard. Hopefully, he's falling down drunk somewhere and never will give the order."

Just then they heard a revolver shot to the

south and then the sound of heavy horse hooves pounding on the hard ground.

"Here they come!" Buckskin bellowed. "Get ready." He pushed Mitzi inside the well house and saw she had a handgun. "Don't shoot it," he said and slammed the door.

The attack came from the south road. Buckskin couldn't figure how many riders. A dozen, maybe more. He could see nothing for two or three minutes, then two rifles nearest the trail blazed hot lead at the attackers. Buckskin aimed down the lane and fired twice, then heard most of the other rifles that could get a line of fire that way begin talking.

Twice he heard cries of pain. One horse went down and he heard the death scream of the animal. The thundering of hooves slowed and then stopped.

No horse had entered the ranch yard. Buckskin fired twice more down the same way, and the other weapons his men held spoke again and again firing blindly into an area. One more scream of pain and protest, then the hooves hit dirt again but this time the sounds became fainter and fainter.

When the sounds trailed off to silence, Buckskin came out from behind the well house and ran forward. "Stay in place," he shouted. "I'm going to take a look."

He held his Spencer repeating rifle ready, a round in the chamber and all set to fire. He walked with as little noise as possible. At first he saw nothing. Then he was thirty yards away from the closest building and he could see dim outlines ahead. Another thirty feet and he saw a horse down at the side of the trail. It wasn't moving. A few feet on, he saw a man sprawled in the middle of the trail.

Buckskin ran up to him but saw clearly a bullet hole in the side of the man's head. Half the top of his scalp had been blasted off by the force of the heavy rifle round.

Buckskin beat down a surge of bile and walked on down the trail. He found two more horses down. One screamed in agony as it sensed someone coming. The animal had both front legs broken and lay pawing the ground.

Buckskin put a .52 caliber Spencer round through the mare's head ending her misery.

He found one more dead horse but no more human bodies.

Five minutes later back in the ranch yard, he reported what he had found to the men. There was a moment of silence and he heard the two hoot owl calls from the north. Still all clear there.

Mitzi came up beside Buckskin. She still carried the handgun, a small framed .32.

"Will they be back?"

"Depends. A lot of first time gunhands don't like the idea of thinking about dying. They lost one man and three horses out there. Gonna make them think hard. Is ten dollars a day worth dying for?"

"Is that what Lamont pays them?"

"Could be. I've seen it as a going wage in a range war. A man can make a lot of money in a month, if he doesn't get killed first."

"I talked to the Attorney General's man. He and Claude were in an upper window with rifles. I heard them shooting into the riders when the rest of you shot."

"Two more rifles will come in handy."

As he said it a rifle spoke from the north and they heard a rifle slug slam into the wall of the ranch house. It had no lights on so the shooter had no real target. Another rifle shot slapped through the air ten yards from them and was gone.

With the first shot, Buckskin had dropped to the ground and pulled Mitzi with him. His hand held one breast as he kept her low to the ground. A moment later he moved his hand.

"Sorry. I had to grab anything I could find."

"Hey, I'm not sorry at all. Reminded me of last night."

"Our job right now is to stay alive. Wonder how Blackhawk is doing to the north?"

"Where the sniper is?"

"If I know Blackhawk, he probably has that sniper's position pinned down by now and is in the process of neutralizing him."

"Making him neutral?"

Buckskin laughed and looked at her in the moonlight. Such a pretty girl. "Something like that. We probably won't have to worry about that one much longer."

A soft shadow showed from around the side of the barn. Buckskin stood and walked that way. "Hey, nobody out, stay in your position."

"Had to take a piss," the shadow's voice said. Almost at the same time a six-gun's hammer cocked back and Buckskin dove to the left drawing his weapon as he fell. The revolver in the shadow man's hand blasted twice, then

Kit Dalton

Buckskin fired twice from where he lay in the ranch yard dust. He heard a wail and the figure rushed to the barn and through the small door.

Buckskin leaped up and chased him. He went through the barn door bent low so he was only two-feet off the floor. When the door opened, two shots slammed through the void above Buckskin. He gave a cry and fell to the left hoping to fool the shooter.

Nothing moved for a long, long sixty seconds. Then Buckskin heard a groan to his left. The horse stalls were that way. He came to his feet silently and edged in that direction. He had four rounds left since he stared with six. No chance to reload.

He moved on silent footpads. Then he waited. The inside of the big barn was as dark as the fifth level of a gold mine at midnight. He breathed shallowly, then held his breath. He could hear someone breathing to his left.

Buckskin wished he could strike a match and throw it, but as soon as it flared he'd be shot. He waited. Something fell. Buckskin wished he had a silent weapon. His knife wasn't in its usual place on his belt. He swept his hand slowly along the first horse stall. Nothing. He moved to the other side and repeated the move and his hand hit something solid.

A handle. He picked it up hoping it was a pitchfork. It was. Three tines. Perfect. He holstered his six-gun and with the fork began a slow, silent probe of the area where he thought he heard the man.

Another groan came farther along the stalls. Buckskin skipped a stall and tested the next one. He could hear someone breathing. Buckskin took another step and the board squeaked in protest at the weight on it.

The flash and report of the six-gun round came almost at the same time, and Buckskin felt the slug tear into his left arm, spin him around and he dropped behind the wall of the next stall. He gritted his teeth to keep from crying out. Make the man think he missed.

Buckskin felt the wound with his right hand. Bleeding like a stuck shoat. He shivered and then set his jaw and picked up the pitchfork again. He had a location. Now he needed a specific target. Silently he took off his left boot and tried to remember the layout of the barn. The outer wall was six feet behind the horse stalls.

He positioned the pitchfork near him, then threw the boot at the wall ten feet away and grabbed the pitchfork. The boot hit the wall and the gunman fired four times. By the time he fired the last shot, at the wall, Buckskin was around the stall partition and lunging forward with the pitchfork like a bayonet.

In the last flash of the six-gun he caught a glimpse of the face behind the weapon. He adjusted his aim and drove forward with the three-tined death machine.

The pitchfork drove into flesh.

Buckskin heard a wail and then a long low moan followed by the deadly sound of the last gush of air out of a dying man's lungs.

Then all was quiet.

Buckskin struck a match and held it low. He hoped the man was Isaiah Lombard, but he wasn't. Buckskin left the pitchfork in place where it had stabbed through the man's chest. One tine drove in about where his heart should be.

He struck another match, found his boot and put it on. He left the barn and called softly for Mitzi. She came.

"Are you all right?"

"Fine, you get back in the house, upstairs in a bedroom. Close the door and lock it and don't let anyone in, not even me. We don't know how many people have infiltrated into the buildings. Any fires yet?"

She shook her head in the moonlight. He bent and kissed her lips then pointed at the house. She held the revolver in her right hand as she ran for the back kitchen door.

"Be on the alert, men," Buckskin bellowed. "We just had one attacker slip in on foot. There may be more. Don't trust anyone on foot, not even me."

He waited then, near the well house.

A moment later a small shed at the outer rim of buildings on the ranch burst into flames.

"Let it burn," Buckskin called. "Stay out of the light. Not anything much of value in there."

He sprinted for the next building, a small barn where they kept some hay and the milk cows and favorite horses in the winter. A vague shape moved against the building's wall. Buckskin couldn't remember if he had a friendly gun in that barn or not. The shadow edged forward, then bent and struck a match.

Buckskin fired three times with his six-gun. To the right and slightly above the flare of the match, a man brayed in pain and slammed backward. The match went out. Buckskin moved forward, soft, short steps toward the man near the barn. He was within ten feet of him when the shot man screamed and fired twice.

Buckskin returned fire and heard the man blubbering, then his breath came short and rattling before it stopped altogether.

He listened again, but heard no more sound from the fire starter. He watched the soft moonlit yard, but saw no movement.

The hoot owl's call came three times, and Buckskin scowled. That was the signal that Blackhawk was in trouble. To the north. Somewhere along the creek. Silently, he reloaded his six-gun with six cartridges, then went around the tool shed and trotted north toward the closest spot the creek came to the ranch buildings.

He'd been there before. This was the place where he had first looked at the Spade Bit only a few days ago. He trotted toward the spot making no attempts to be quiet. He entered the fringes of the brush and crouched low.

"Blackhawk, you all right?" Buckskin called. He ducked lower and heard the six-gun blast not twenty feet from him to the front and slightly to the right.

"Do not return any fire, Buckskin Morgan. I have your friend here as my shield. You try to shoot me, you kill him. He isn't as good an Indian as he once was. Drop your weapons, even your hideout and walk forward with your hands in the air. When I hear you close enough I'll light my coal oil torch and check you. If you try anything, anything at all, Blackhawk is one dead Indian."

Buckskin didn't reply. He worked to the left and forward on his belly, not making a sound. He crawled with his elbows and knees, moving ahead slowly, his Colt out in front and cocked so he wouldn't have to give away his position before he shot.

Two minutes later, the voice came again. "No tricks, Buckskin. If you don't recognize my voice, I'm Isaiah Lombard and I don't have a damn thing to lose by killing this Indian and you and half the people at the ranch. So you come out with your hands high."

Again, Buckskin didn't respond. He found a patch of moonlight ahead. It was a small clearing and evidently Lombard and Blackhawk were directly across it. How could he cover the distance and not be seen?

He wished that he had one of his small dynamite bombs. Sure would be handy. His hands and elbows touched river rocks. The stream bed had come this way at one time and left rounded stones the size of baseballs.

Buckskin considered it. He picked up a dozen of the baseball-sized rocks, got on his knees and hefted them. He needed a precise target. He tossed one of the stones into the air so it would come down a dozen feet to his right.

He fisted another rock at once. His stone hit the brush and clattered to the ground. Lombard fired twice into the area where the rock hit and Buckskin had his target. He threw the heavy rocks hard. He was less than fifteen feet from the fugitive.

Buckskin threw the rocks as fast as he could get them in his hand. The first one evidently missed, the second brought a wail of surprise, and the third and fourth zeroed in on the voice. Lombard screamed in pain, then wailed. He fired the last four shots from his six-gun and screamed and cursed. Then he stood in the faint moonlight and ran forward into the open place and fired a hide-out twice.

The derringer barked like a .45 caliber, then was empty.

Buckskin called to him. "Lombard, I have you in my sights. Give up or die. Take your choice. Did you hurt Blackhawk?"

"Killed the son-of-a-bitching Indian."

Buckskin screamed in anger and fired four times. Lombard went down with three slugs in his chest. He never moved in the early evening moonlight once he sprawled on the ground.

Buckskin rushed past him to the spot where he had first heard the man talk. He lit two matches and saw Blackhawk on the ground, his hands and feet tied and a gag in his mouth. Buckskin burned his fingers on the match but got the gag off.

Blackhawk growled and spit and tried to see Buckskin in the faint moonlight.

"Okay, okay, so he surprised me. I'm an Indian. That doesn't mean that I'm a good Indian. I was raised by you damn white-eyes, why should I be any better in the woods than you?"

The two laughed and then hushed.

"Any more of them out here?"

"He had two men with him. Planned on sending them in right after the cavalry charge and burn every building in the place."

"They didn't quite make it," Buckskin said. "Let's get back to the ranch and see if they have had any more trouble. Also, I'd like to get this arm bandaged up. I caught a round."

Back in the kitchen, Mitzi put some healing salve on his wound. The bullet had gone in and out of his upper left arm. It would be sore and not much good for a week or two.

All was still quiet at the ranch. The Attorney General's man came downstairs and looked at the three dead attackers, then went with Buckskin and checked out Lombard.

By midnight, Buckskin figured the threat was over. He put half the men on guard and let the other half sleep. He wandered the ranch buildings until dawn, then went in for a cup of coffee.

Mitzi came over from the kitchen range with a pot of coffee. She waved at Buckskin and hurried over to where Jody stood and kissed him on the cheek. He beamed.

"Looks like it's all over," Buckskin said. Everyone knew that Isaiah Lombard was dead.

The Attorney General's man nodded. "Seems like Mr. Lombard will no longer be lording it over the citizens of Ada county."

Jody looked up. "These four dead bodies we have, any problems with that?"

"They attacked your ranch, you were defending it. I'd say that's a plain case of self-defense if I've ever heard of one. I'll take care of it with the county authorities. We will need you to sign statements about the deaths for the record."

Mitzi beamed. "Well, it looks like things are settled. I just want to thank all of you for your help. Especially you, Buckskin Morgan and Harry Blackhawk. If it hadn't been for you two, this ranch would now belong to Isaiah Lombard."

She smiled. "I think now is a good time to announce it, don't you, Jody?"

He nodded, grinned sheepishly and looked down at his boots.

"Jody has asked me to marry him and I said yes. The wedding will be in two weeks. You're all invited."

They all congratulated the smiling couple. Then Mitzi offered the two men beds in the bunkhouse and the promise of a good breakfast even if they slept to noon.

They waved and walked to the bunkhouse. Blackhawk looked at Buckskin. "You won't tell them about how Lombard caught me by surprise?"

"No reason. I figure since you're going to build me a great new saddle, least I can do is not tell your deep dark secret."

"A new saddle?"

"About the size of it. With some fancy tooling and maybe a spot or two of silver trim."

Blackhawk took a fake swing at him and they walked on to the bunkhouse. Now that the tension was over, both of them realized that they were so tired they couldn't talk straight.

Buckskin stretched out on a bunk. He decided that he'd take the train back to Denver for a couple of weeks to recover and relax. After that he'd look for a new assignment. He wondered what it might be and where the next detective job would take him.